Lust in the Stacks

NATALIE FALKENWRATH

BENTON HOUSE PUBLISHING

Benton House Publishing

bentonhousepublishing.com

ISBN 978-1-952057-00-7 (Paperback)

ISBN 9781952057038 (eBook)

For more information about the author and

upcoming books, please visit

nataliefalkenwrath.com

To coworkers of a past life,

thanks for all you've given me

Chapter 1

Alex knew she wasn't fired, but she sure felt like she'd been fired. *Banished.* Alexandria Rossi was one of many tech support staff in the Cowling University IT department. Alex had always enjoyed her job at CUIT. She liked her small blue-gray cube in the lower levels of the massive student union. The student union was the heart of Cowling, and CUIT was tucked neatly into one of the ventricles. It thrummed with the pulse of campus life. From the monotony of daily coursework to the excitement over special events to the stress of finals, it was all felt in the student union. Students and faculty filtered through, bringing all the flavors of academia with them. At her desk, alongside the cubes of her coworkers, Alex was in the center of it all. Or at least she used to be.

Today Alex had been reassigned. She was being sent to work in the smallest library on the farthest edge of campus. Sent to be the only tech geek in a sea of librarians. And not just any librarians - *humanities* librarians. The most librarian-y librarians of all. Alex knew she would never feel at home there.

Alex took a second to fix her ponytail, sweeping errant brown waves out of her face, as she looked wistfully around her near-empty cube. She'd felt at home here. Alex hated the idea of moving. She had been sitting at this desk in this cube for almost three years. That was the longest Alex had ever done any job. And she did it well. At central CUIT, students and staff came to her for help with their many technical problems. Most of their issues were easy to solve, and Alex would fix them with a wry smile and witty comment. *Do librarians like smart-asses like me? Will they get my jokes? Do librarians even smile?* When Alex pictured librarians, she pictured pinch-faced old ladies with their lips puckered in a permanent '*shush.*'

"Ugh, this sucks," Alex bemoaned to her 'office husband' and best work friend, Charles. He was a big guy with gold-blonde curls and a knack for telling stories that left Alex in stitches. Charles was sitting in

Alex's cube, watching her pack. He was offering her a whole lot less sympathy than she felt she deserved. "I can't believe I'm being sent away like this. Out to pasture like a dying horse."

"I don't think that's what 'out to pasture' means," Charles said with a snort, rolling his eyes as he lazily played with her *Slinky*.

"Shut up. You know what I mean," Alex pouted, snatching the toy from his hand and throwing it into the box. "I think Geoff is torturing me on purpose. He hates me."

Geoff, their boss and the director of CUIT, was a complete tool. How he'd gotten the job was a complete mystery to Alex. Geoff knew next to nothing about computers and somehow even less about how to motivate employees. He was a my-way-or-the-highway manager, choosing more often than not, to follow his 'gut' rather than listen to those under him. The whole department found him insufferable. Alex was just the only one stupid enough to let it show. She'd rolled her eyes at his pointless pontificating one too many times. And now she was paying for it.

"Geoff doesn't hate you," Charles said. He was utterly unconvincing; he could hardly look at her as he said it. Alex groaned loudly.

"I've been banished!" she all but yelled. Alex dropped the last dusty trinket into the box and wiped her hands on her jeans. "Banished, Charles!"

"Don't think of it as being 'banished,' think of it as a vote of confidence - somebody has to run the backup-migration project; we have to touch every computer. Geoff trusts you to do it out there on your own."

Charles was so full of shit, and he knew it. This move had nothing whatsoever to do with trust. It was a punishment, Alex had no doubt.

"Dude, like you said, we have to touch *every* computer on campus. There are plenty of computers *here* I could be 'touching.'" Alex wiggled her fingers.

"And plenty of techs here too," Charles countered.

"Fine, but if he *had* to send me somewhere, did it have to be *there*? There are so many buildings that are more interesting and more central than the effing *humanities* library. If he 'trusted' me, he could have assigned me to the *biggest* library. At least it's just across the street. But no. He hates me so, I get sent to the boonies. Alone. This is banishment. Plain and simple."

"Fine, if you're determined to be pissy about it, be pissy about it." Charles rolled his eyes toward the ceiling.

"I will. Thank you." Alex inclined her head to Charles. She knew she was acting crabby, but she felt justified in her indignation. Alex took a deep sigh and looked around her cube. "Well, I guess that's everything."

"Want me to drive you over there?" Charles offered, but Alex shook her head.

"No, thanks. If you did, then I'd just have to walk back to my car after work," she sighed. "So, I guess I should say my goodbyes here."

"Bye, Alex." Charles stood and patted her on the back as she walked past him. Alex stopped at the doorway and turned back. She didn't want to go.

"This blows," she whined, looking at Charles sadly. "I'm never going to see anybody ever again."

"Not true, you'll still have to come over once a week for the check-in meeting," Charles pointed out.

"Oh, great," Alex scoffed. She hated that pointless waste-of-time meeting, and Charles very well knew that. "I can't wait to make that the highlight of my week."

"All this complaining is really going to make me miss you," Charles said sarcastically as he settled into his own desk chair.

"Shut up, you know you'll miss me, bi-boy." Charles was not only her designated 'work husband' but also the only other queer person in the department. They were the gay-namic duo. Alex, the super lesbian, and her bi-boy Charlie. They had been attached at the hip since Alex joined the department. And now they were being split up.

"I can't miss you if you never leave." Charles looked at the clock. "Hey, don't you have a meeting over there in like ten minutes?"

"Shit, yeah. I gotta run. I'll message you all the gory details."

Alex was huffing and puffing by the time she reached her dreaded destination. Alex scowled up at the letters carved over the ancient wooden doors. 'Cowling University Library for the Humanities.' *It's so pathetic it doesn't even get its own name.* All the other libraries had names. Benton, Johnson, Butler-Pierce. But not this little old thing. *Pathetic.* From the outside, it hardly looked like a library. More like a repurposed presidents' mansion or something. It was shabby and ancient. Even the outside seemed somehow dusty.

Let's get this over with. Alex pushed her way inside. Nancy, the library's administrative assistant, was waiting just inside, looking impatient. Alex glanced at her watch; she was very late. Nancy must have been waiting a while for her.

"Sorry I'm late, I didn't realize how bad parking was going to be," Alex wheezed, exaggerating her need to catch her breath just a bit. "I should really work out more. Although if parking is always this bad, I guess I won't need to." She grinned.

"Uh-huh." Nancy raised an eyebrow and gave Alex a quick once-over. Nancy was a thin middle-aged woman with limp graying hair and glasses that made her eyes 'pop' in all the wrong ways. Alex had only met her once before. She was a bit serious but otherwise seemed innocuous enough. She didn't look like she was going to 'shush' Alex in any case.

"Do you need me to carry anything?" Nancy asked. Alex was loaded down, wearing her backpack, with a messenger bag slung across her chest, and a box in her arms. The load seemed to grow increasingly heavy the longer she stood there.

"No, I'm good," Alex shifted her weight. The backpack straps were digging into her shoulders and pushing the messenger bag up to her neck. It was painfully uncomfortable, but Alex liked to think of herself as tough and self-reliant. It wouldn't do her macho techie self-image any good to ask for help carrying a box of office toys.

"Alright then, follow me." Nancy led Alex in through the library, zig-zagging through the stacks. *This cannot be the most direct route to anywhere!* Just as Alex thought her arms might actually fall off, Nancy finally stopped at a door and opened it to reveal Alex's new office.

"Wait, I get a whole office?" Alex blinked in astonishment.

"Yes, *you* do," Nancy said in a tone that told Alex, Nancy did not have an office of her own. Alex set down her box and wriggled free of her bags. She rolled her shoulders as she looked around the little room.

The office was a perfect square of white walls, broken up only by the door which took up the left third of one wall. A long black desk ran the length of the wall opposite the door; pushed into it was a basic black desk chair. The office didn't have any windows. There was so much empty wall space; Alex's mind immediately went to covering one of the walls with computer monitors *Hackers* style. *This could be pretty sweet*, she thought. It was the first positive thought she'd had about her new post. Alex decided she was going to make the most of this one perk.

"If you want to leave your stuff here, I can give you a little tour of the Cowling Library for the Humanities," Nancy chirped.

"Okay, let's get a *moooo*ve on then," Alex grinned. Nancy stared blankly back at her. "You know, Cowling, cow, moo?" Alex explained her terrible attempt at humor.

"Oh, I've never heard that one before. Funny," Nancy said without the slightest hint of humor in her voice. *That stupid shit usually goes over better, at least at CUIT.* Alex made a mental note to reign in the bad jokes until the library folks knew her a little better.

Nancy proceeded to walk Alex through the library, from one space to another through the stacks. The air in the stacks was stagnant and smelled of dust and old books. Alex felt like an archaeologist wandering through ancient tombs. She almost felt like she should be carrying a torch. *This place is kind of creepy.* When Nancy wasn't talking, it was quiet as death; the only sounds were their soft footsteps on the carpeted floor and the buzz of the fluorescent lights overhead. Each row of stacks had its own little light switch that Nancy would tap as they wove their way through. Light on, walk through, light off. Next row. Light on, walk through, light off.

Is she taking the most circuitous route possible just to mess with me? There was no way in hell that Alex would be able to find her way back to her office on her own. There was also no way she was going to admit just how turned-around she was. So, Alex went along with the tour and made plans to do her own solo exploration tomorrow. *If I ever find my way out tonight.*

Nancy showed Alex a cozy book-lined reading room, the dusty and secluded archives, and several cave-like computer labs. The spaces had a museum-like quality to them, each quieter and more dimly lit than the last. *Are there literally zero windows in this library?* It struck Alex that in the event of a fire, she would have no idea how to escape. That was a *fun* thought. Nancy led Alex upstairs to the staff offices and break room.

"Most of us eat lunch here," Nancy said when they entered the break room. "But not all at once," she hastened to add.

"Charming," Alex muttered.

The break room was tiny, and boy, was it *bleak*. While all the other library common spaces had been decorated with art or covered with bookshelves, here, the grey walls were all but bare. There was a dingy little kitchenette with two lop-sided tables surrounded by a slew of mismatched chairs. A metal storage cabinet stood against one wall and a 1970s lime-green sofa against the wall opposite. It was depressing as hell.

The last stop on Nancy's tour, presented as the *pièce de résistance* of the whole library, was the 'research desk.' It was large and intricately carved - an *antique*. It was here that librarians took shifts answering questions and guiding their patrons in their studies. Nancy gave Alex a long, gushing history lesson about the desk, but Alex didn't hear a word she said. Because standing at that oak monstrosity was one of the most beautiful women Alex had ever seen in her life.

Nancy called her Cait Murphy. Alex called her *gorgeous*. She was far and away, the most pleasing sight Alex had laid eyes on since stepping through the library's heavy doors. Cait was the very definition of 'sexy librarian.' She was dressed in a dark green sweater and tan corduroy skirt, but her body looked made to wear lingerie. She was all long limbs and smooth curves. Cait's shimmering copper hair fell to her waist, just above where the arch of her back met the roundness of her ass. Cait stepped toward her, and Alex quickly shifted her eyes from Cait's body to her face.

Freckles were sprinkled like fairy dust across Cait's porcelain white skin. Her light eyelashes made her green eyes stand out like jewels in her face. And her lips… *Oh god, her lips*. They were pouting and plump and perfect. Alex blinked. *Her lips are talking to me. Shit.*

"…that makes the most sense, d'ya think?" Cait asked. *Where is that accent from?*

"Alex?" Nancy's voice snapped Alex into focus.

"What?" she asked dumbly.

"Does that make sense?" Cait repeated. Alex had no idea what Cait had said, therefore no idea if it made any sense whatsoever, but she nodded anyway.

"Yeah, sure," Alex nodded.

"Great, see you tomorrow then," Cait's face broke into a dazzling smile, and Alex almost fainted. *Holy shit, she's pretty*. Alex regained enough of her mental faculties to stop staring at Cait and follow Nancy back through the stacks to her office. If she hadn't been paying attention to her surroundings before, they were totally forgotten now. Alex's mind was entirely consumed by the ginger goddess she'd just met.

You have a girlfriend, she tried to remind herself. *Cait's just a coworker*. Alex wondered how closely she would be working with Cait. She had been standing at the research desk; that meant she's probably an actual librarian. *So much for wrinkled old ladies*. Alex wondered if Cait worked there every day. She'd said, 'see you tomorrow,' so it seemed likely.

"Does everybody here work the same schedule?" Alex asked.

"I'm off now," Nancy said, looking at her watch. "I work from seven to four, so I'm out an hour earlier than the rest. But otherwise, yes."

"You mean half-an-hour, right?" Alex asked.

"Oh no, the library is open from eight to midnight, so there are two shifts: eight-to-five and five-to-midnight. Most of the staff work eight to five. Didn't you already know that?" Nancy looked at her curiously. "I assumed you did since Geoff said you would be working the same hours."

"Eight-to-*five*?" Alex asked, horrified.

"Yes, exactly," Nancy must have read Alex's expression because she looked sympathetically back at her. "You can take an extra coffee break if you'd like."

"Oh, okay," Alex said. Inside she was screaming. *An extra half hour? I get moved to the shithole middle of nowhere library and have to work an additional half-hour each day? Fuck that.* Even the eye-candy that was Cait couldn't make up for the extra two-and-a-half hours a week she'd be working for precisely *zero* dollars increased pay. Alex considered sending a strongly worded email to Geoff, voicing her displeasure. *Isn't that the sort of thing that got me stuck here in the first place?*

"Have a good evening," Nancy dropped Alex back at her office and disappeared into the stacks.

Alex sat down at her desk. She spun in her office chair for a few rotations while taking stock of her situation. There were exactly *two* upsides to working here in the library: her very own office and the very hot librarian. Alex contemplated how she could make the most of both. She already had plans for her office. She was going to build herself a geek den that would have Charles panting with envy. But there wasn't much to be 'done' regarding Cait, aside from appreciating the view.

Alex and her girlfriend Jasmine weren't in the best place relationship-wise. Some days, Alex felt like they were on the slowest road to break-up in the history of the world. And yet, Jasmine was still her girlfriend, and Alex loved her.

Alex and Jasmine had been together for well over a year now. But at some point, the relationship had stalled. Sometime around when Alex had tried and failed to get Jasmine to move in with her, things had changed. Over the last few months, Alex felt like they'd barely been a 'couple' at all. They texted daily, sure. But their dates were few and far between and tended to end in chaste kisses and quick farewells. Now and then, Alex would manage to get Jasmine's shirt off. If she was very, very lucky, they'd even get each other off. But that was it.

As frustrating as the state of their relationship was, Alex loved Jasmine. And Alex would never cheat on her. That wasn't the type of person she was. So when it came to the question of Cait, Alex knew library eye-candy would have to remain just that, eye-candy. All looking and no touching.

Alex took out her ponytail and rubbed the back of her head. Rather than dwell on the sexy temptress in a corduroy skirt, Alex decided to put her plans for her office into motion. She set up her laptop and messaged Charles, asking him to meet her over lunch tomorrow. She wanted his help ransacking the back storerooms of CUIT.

One upside to having a boss who didn't have a clue, was that CUIT techs in the know had pretty much free range over all inventory of old equipment - the tech pulled from the most recent classroom and office upgrades. Computer equipment at Cowling U. was routinely upgraded every five years. That meant pulling out and replacing plenty of perfectly good monitors and CPUs. Eventually, they would be recycled, but in the intermediary, they sat in storage.

And as a member of CUIT, Alex had access to all of it. Alex was going to totally geek-out her office. She steepled her fingers like a *Bond* villain as she pictured it. *Excellent, excellent.* Charles would surely be jealous, but what would the librarians think? Too geeky?

"I wonder if Cait likes geeks," Alex said aloud to herself. *Hell, does she even like women?* Alex thought that she might; she didn't have any reason to believe so, but she did. *Not that it really matters, it's not like I'm gonna ask her out. Look, don't touch.* Alex sighed and pulled out her phone to text her girlfriend.

'I get out of work in 30. You available tonight?' Alex put away her phone and picked a trinket from her little toybox. A tiny lion, the university mascot, holding a miniature pride flag. She put it on the desk next to her computer. She absent-mindedly wondered where Cait's office was and if it would contain any clues as to her 'preferences.'

'I could meet for dinner. Falafel place at 7.' Jasmine replied. *Ah, the falafel place.* It was Jasmine's favorite. Despite being a white girl from the suburbs, she really 'connected' with the culture behind her name. It was sometimes obnoxious, but Alex really loved falafel, so she didn't ever argue when Jasmine suggested it.

'Ok, see u there.'

Alex gave herself a solid ten minutes to dig her way out of the labyrinthian stacks. It took thirteen. *I need to make a map.* Otherwise, she'd spend that extra thirty minutes a day at work just finding her way to and from her office. *I guess there are worse ways to spend my time*, Alex mused, *I could actually be doing work.*

Chapter 2

Whenever Alex forgot why she was with Jasmine, it only took seconds in her presence to remind her. Jasmine was beautiful and so fucking *cool*. When Alex arrived, Jasmine was sitting at the small middle eastern restaurant, a book in one hand, a tiny cup of espresso in the other. Her bright red lipstick was striking on her otherwise make-up-free face. Everything surrounding Jasmine, from her clothes to her notebook, to the teal bike waiting outside, was a statement. Usually retro or vintage - always just the right amount of wear to be authentically aged but not shabby. Even her long dirty-blonde hair was at once casually messy and utterly alluring. She made it all look *effortless*. Like she'd rolled out of bed, threw on some lipstick, and was instantly queen of the city.

"Hey girl, anybody ever tell you, you put the *hip* in hipster?" Alex pulled out the chair opposite Jasmine and sat down. Jasmine arched one full eyebrow at her.

"Only you, Alex," she said with a slight shake of her head. She carefully bookmarked her page and set down the book. "I already ordered, I assumed you would want the same thing you *always* get."

"You say that like you don't get the same thing every time, too," Alex said. They both ordered the same falafel plate. That's why they came here. That and the hummus.

"Did I tell you I got reassigned to the Cowling Library for the Humanities today?" Alex asked as she and Jasmine ate. "It sucks, but I got my own office."

"Yes, Alex, you told the *whole world*. It's on your *Insta*."

"That's not the 'whole world,'" Alex rolled her eyes.

"I'm just saying," Jasmine continued. "This seems like a big deal. You could have texted me separately. I hate hearing about my girlfriend's life via social media like some *rando*."

You don't text me any more than I text you. The only difference is that you also don't post to social media, Alex thought, but she bit her tongue. Jasmine had been growing colder and more distant lately; in a way, it felt good that Jasmine even cared enough to scold her for posting online before telling her.

"Sorry," Alex rubbed her leg against Jasmine's under the table. "I'll tell you first next time. It is kind of a big deal, I mean, I've been *banished*, you know."

"You're so dramatic." Jasmine shook her head, dismissively.

"You say that because you haven't seen it. It's so old and dark. Even Morticia Adams would be like, 'Woah, this is depressing AF! Can we get at least get a window up in this bitch?'" Alex grinned at Jasmine, but her girlfriend didn't seem to find Alex's description amusing in the least. Alex shrugged. "Besides which, there's absolutely nothing around that part of campus. Not a single decent coffee shop. There isn't even really anywhere to park."

"You could try not driving everywhere," Jasmine snorted. "To think, maybe this little *inconvenience* could actually get you to stop contributing to global climate change. I mean, listening to me is apparently not doing the trick."

Alex shoved a mouthful of falafel into her face and said nothing. They'd had this argument before, and she didn't want to go over it again. Alex was not 'cycling' for an hour through traffic and midwestern winters to appease Jasmine. It wasn't like she drove some gas-guzzling SUV, her tiny car was about as efficient as they got.

There was a long pause while they both just sat and chewed. The food was good, too good to allow Alex to be grumpy. They chatted about Jasmine's day for a while before falling into a companionable silence. It was nice enough, but Alex was itching for a little more than 'companionability' from her supposed girlfriend.

"So, do you have any plans after dinner?" Alex asked. She scooped up a bit of stray hummus and slowly licked it off her finger.

"Alex…" Jasmine began with notable impatience.

"Maybe you could come back to my place for a bit. It's been a while..." Alex repeated the action, this time taking her sweet time, sucking her finger clean. *Mmmmm.*

"Why do you always have to do this?" Jasmine sat back and looked at her with an exasperated expression.

"Do what?"

"Make every date about sex."

"Who said anything about *sex*?" Alex feigned innocence. Of course, she was thinking about sex. How was Jasmine *not* thinking about sex? It had been so damn long.

"Alexandria Rossi, don't you play dumb with me. You've been practically vibrating in your seat all night." Jasmine tilted her head. "And stop licking your damn finger."

"Okay, fine." Alex wiped her hands with her napkin and tossed it onto the table. "But is it really so bad that I want to have sex with my girlfriend?"

"No, I didn't say that it was."

"It's been a long time since you've been Jas-*mine*." Alex grinned at Jasmine and wiggled her eyebrows suggestively. Jasmine let out a long, what-am-I-going-to-do-with-you sigh.

"Fine. I'll come back with you," she said, catching Alex's eye. "But I am not promising *anything*," she added, her lips carefully forming each word; her tongue visible against her teeth as she pronounced '*thing.*' Alex knew what it meant when Jasmine used that tone of voice. *She's thinking about sex too.* Alex tried to suppress her grin while inside her head, she sang, '*I'm gonna bang my girlfriend, I'm gonna bang my girlfriend.*'

Alex hadn't planned for having Jasmine over in advance, so she knew her apartment was a total disaster. But lucky for Alex, Jasmine was a single-speed bike riding hipster. And that gave Alex time. While Jasmine cycled her way through the city, Alex raced home ahead of her. Alex shoved her dirty laundry in the closet, loaded the dishwasher, and generally made the place look as if she hadn't spent all her spare time in the last few days eating ramen and playing video games like a college student. She even remembered to light Jasmine's favorite candles just in time.

"I'm so glad you came over," Alex grinned as she opened the door for Jasmine.

"It has been a while," Jasmine smiled faintly. "I'm glad you asked me. Can I put my leftovers in your fridge?"

"Only you would have leftover falafel," Alex teased. "Be careful, or I might eat it while your back is turned."

"Not everybody likes to stuff themselves until they look pregnant," Jasmine shook her head as she packed away the food.

"I do not look pregnant," Alex muttered. She rubbed at her belly. *Do I?*

Jasmine helped herself to a glass of wine.

Alex leaned on the counter. She watched her girlfriend sip the deep red liquid. Jasmine looked like a model in her high-waisted jeans and crop-top, her long wavy hair down over one shoulder. Jasmine was cool, and she knew it. Alex looked down at her own jeans and Cowling University t-shirt and sighed inwardly. She wasn't cool, not by a long shot. Alex knew that she had a nice enough body. She was trim, with small but perky breasts and softly curving hips. She was *attractive*. But that didn't make her a match for Jasmine. Jasmine had something else; some better-than-you air about her that made her seem almost untouchably hip. And yet so *touchable*.

Alex looked seductively at her girlfriend. Jasmine gave her the tiniest hint of a smile. Encouraged, Alex pulled Jasmine in by her belt loops and kissed her. Jasmine returned the kiss, but she was holding back, not committing fully to the action. Alex took the wine glass from Jasmine's hand and set it down on the counter. She kissed her again. This time Jasmine kissed her back with full intensity. Jasmine was an excellent kisser. Alex held her face in her hands and kissed her again and again. Jasmine bit her lip encouragingly, and Alex felt heat ignite between her legs.

Alex pushed up Jasmine's shirt, and Jasmine ducked her head to allow Alex to take it off completely. The black lace bralette she had on underneath was sexy as hell. Alex felt the heat and desire spreading from her center out through her entire body. She gently kneaded one of Jasmine's breasts. Alex could feel Jasmine's nipple stiffen under the thin fabric. Alex pinched it lightly, and Jasmine moaned. *She seems really into it today*. The heat between Alex's legs began to throb.

Alex grabbed Jasmine's ass with both hands and pulled her close. Jasmine moved her hips, grinding hungrily on Alex. Through their jeans, she could feel the pressure of Jasmine's pelvic bone on hers. Jasmine *is definitely horny*. Alex briefly wondered if Jasmine had known so back at the restaurant when she was playing hard to get. Alex decided she didn't care. What mattered was what happened next.

Alex grinned as she hurriedly unbuttoned Jasmine's pants. She slid one hand down inside, letting her fingers slip between Jasmine's legs, probing. *Oh god, she's soaking.* Encouraged, Alex pulled Jasmine's pants and panties down and off. Then she lifted her girlfriend onto the counter. Alex rubbed two fingers along Jasmine's slick opening while her thumb pressed lightly on her clit. Jasmine arched her hips toward Alex's hand. Alex slid one finger inside, then a second. Jasmine was moaning loudly now, half-way to screaming as Alex worked in and out of her with increasing speed.

"Oh god," Jasmine shuddered, and Alex felt the pulsing tightness around her fingers. Jasmine leaned forward.

"Let's move to the sofa," Jasmine whispered. Alex pulled away and followed Jasmine to the soft gray couch, pulling her own shirt off along the way. Jasmine laid on her back along the length of the sofa, legs spread. Alex took a moment to appreciate the view. *She is hot, and she really does know it.* The unattended to heat between Alex's legs throbbed again, begging for attention. But before Alex could remove her pants, Jasmine pulled her down. Jasmine kissed her once before pushing on Alex's shoulders in a not-so-subtle hint that she wanted Alex to go down on her. Alex was happy to oblige, ignoring her own body's desires and kissing a path down Jasmine's stomach, past the small patch of dark hair.

She settled herself between Jasmine's thighs and flicked Jasmine's clit with her tongue. Jasmine moaned and pulled Alex's head in deeper. Alex didn't mind one bit; she loved the smell of her, the taste of her. She could spend hours there. But it didn't take that long; it never did. Jasmine came hard and loud, arching her back and screaming. Her legs tensed, twitching with the aftershocks of orgasm. Slowly she relaxed and released Alex from her grip.

"Was that good?" Alex asked, grinning up at her. It was a rhetorical question. Obviously, it was good. Jasmine laughed.

"Oh, yeah," she sighed contentedly and closed her legs. "Thank you."

"You're welcome," Alex wiped the cum from her face. Jasmine closed her eyes and turned sideways on the sofa. "Hey, now, you're not going to fall asleep on me, are you?" Alex prodded her.

"Sorry, that was just so… *lovely*," Jasmine yawned. She *was* going to fall asleep.

"Seriously?" Alex pouted; she was incredibly turned-on and hoping for at least a little reciprocation.

"Sorry, Lexie. You're just too good," Jasmine smiled but didn't open her eyes. Alex sat back. She was still wearing her bra and jeans. *Jasmine didn't even take my shirt off; I did that*. Alex could feel herself getting annoyed, the muscles in her neck and jaw tense.

"Fine, you fall asleep. I'm going to bed," Alex huffed. Jasmine didn't stir or open her eyes.

"Okay," she whispered back, sleepily as if she hadn't noticed Alex's pissy tone. *Ugh, fine*. Alex stomped off to her room. She flopped down on the bed, thrust her hand into her pants, and took care of her body's need for release on her own. When she was done, she relaxed, her annoyance with Jasmine fading away. Alex was teetering on the edge of sleep when Jasmine appeared at the door.

"Am I too late?" she asked, standing there in her bralette and panties.

"Yeah, a little," Alex sighed.

"I'm sorry," Jasmine climbed into bed and snuggled up against Alex. She didn't actually sound sorry. But Alex couldn't be angry so soon after cumming. She didn't have the energy. Alex put her arms around Jasmine and breathed in the familiar scent of patchouli and jasmine.

"I love you," Alex kissed Jasmine's forehead.

"I love you, too." Jasmine absently traced lines along Alex's bare stomach with her finger. Alex closed her eyes. Sleep began to creep in on her once again.

"I think we should see other people," Jasmine said suddenly.

"What?" Alex lifted her head, instantly wide awake.

"I think we should see other people," Jasmine repeated. The words hit Alex like an icy wave, instantly chilling her to her core. Alex lay there in shock, hardly able to breathe.

"Are you... breaking up with me?" she asked slowly, the words coming out in a hoarse whisper. Jasmine continued to casually run her fingers along the skin of Alex's abdomen.

"No, Lexie. That's the thing," she said with a wistful sigh. "I don't *want* to break up with you… I *love* you… but I also want to see other people."

"Like an open relationship?" Alex asked, numbly. *Is this a dream?* It didn't feel real.

"Yeah, something like that," Jasmine said. "Some people call it 'ethical non-monogamy,' and I think it could be good for us."

"How?"

Jasmine twisted Alex's hair around her finger. Alex lay frozen as she waited for Jasmine to respond. *How could seeing other people possibly be good for us?*

"I just feel like I could appreciate what you give me more if I wasn't trying to get everything from you," Jasmine said finally. Alex knew it wasn't a dream now because it hurt too much. *Ouch.* Alex did her best to give Jasmine everything she asked for and then some. Alex had put more effort into this relationship than any other she'd ever had.

"What am I not giving you? I just-"

"Alex," Jasmine interrupted. "This isn't meant as a criticism of *you*. It's about *me*."

"It has to be at least a little about me," Alex countered. *She says she doesn't want to break up, so why does it feel like she doesn't want to be together either?*

"Well, do you think I'm giving you everything you need out of a *relationship*?" Jasmine asked, her fingers lingering on Alex's stomach, brushing back and forth, just above the waistband of her underpants. The implication was clear enough. *No*, Alex thought, *not tonight anyway. Or last night. Or the night before...* Alex honestly couldn't remember the last time she felt fully satisfied with their sex life. But that was only one tiny aspect of their relationship. She still loved Jasmine, and she was willing to deal with a less-than-ideal sex life. As long as they had a relationship, as long as they loved each other.

"I suppose you're right," Alex agreed quietly. Her heart ached as she said it.

"So doesn't it make sense to try something that might help us both be happier?" Jasmine said logically, not noticing the hurt in Alex's tone.

"Okay, I guess." Alex didn't know what else to say; Jasmine sounded so confident in this choice. Alex knew that if she didn't agree, she was going to lose Jasmine entirely. And she wasn't ready for that.

"Thanks for being so understanding," Jasmine gave Alex a soft peck on the lips. Then she curled up and fell promptly asleep. Alex laid in bed, thinking about what had just happened. *How could this possibly be good? It has to be just another step down the road of the world's slowest breakup.* Alex didn't want an open relationship - *ethical non-monogamy* - but she didn't want to break up either. *What choice do I have?* Alex squeezed her eyes closed and tried not to cry.

Lust in the Stacks

Chapter 3

Alex drove into work the next morning as if in a fog. Jasmine had really meant it. She wanted to see other people. But not break up. Alex still didn't feel like she had any choice but to agree. The only alternative was to split. And Alex wasn't ready for that. She loved Jasmine too much to lose her completely. Alex barely slept thinking about it. Her dreams were filled with visions of other women kissing Jasmine, holding her hand, making her laugh. Other women between her girlfriend's legs.

It was all Alex could think about as she parked her car and stumbled half-asleep into the library. *How is this going to work? Will we tell each other about other people? How many people is she planning on seeing?*

If she sleeps with other people, we have to go back to getting tested. Alex's stomach turned. *Oh god, I have to stop thinking about this.*

Alex looked around. She'd been so lost in her head, she'd wandered through the stacks in completely the wrong direction. Instead of standing outside her office, she was at the bottom of a stairwell. *Shit. Where am I?* If memory served, these stairs led up to the breakroom. *Maybe they'll have coffee.* Alex needed coffee, given how little sleep she'd gotten the night before.

Alex trudged up the stairs. The moment Alex opened the door to the break room, she regretted it. There was coffee in that sad gray space. But there were also four librarians - all older women, all *delighted* to meet Alex. They were almost *manically* friendly in their oddly insistent chit-chat. *They don't get out much, do they?*

One long hour and two terrible cups of coffee later, Alex managed to tear herself away from Dianne, Trisha, Joan, and… *Crap, I already forgot the name of the other one. Big-glasses-wearing librarian.* There had been no sign of the sexy librarian, Cait. *How many librarians can this tiny library possibly need?*

Alex spent the rest of the morning hiding in her office, answering emails, closing neglected tech support tickets, and trying to forget about Jasmine. The best distraction she could think of was to move on her plans to make the absolute most of her bare little office.

'Hey, still up for helping me grab some old monitors and shit from storage over lunch?' Alex messaged Charles.

'Remind me, why are we doing this again?' he replied.

'Gotta pimp my office, bro.'

'You were serious about that? You're such a dork.'

'I can pick up sandwiches on the way over.' *It never hurts to add a little incentive to ensure full cooperation.*

'See you at noon!'

Alex arrived early. It took a little longer than expected, but she and Charles were able to locate all the things she would need to create her perfect little geek cave. While they dug through the dusty storage shelves, Alex filled Charles in on the details of her first day of banishment. Charles clearly thought she was being overly dramatic again.

"Have you ever even *been* to the humanities library?" Alex asked. "It's legit scary. It's like the haunted house at the beginning of *Ghostbusters*, stuffed with the labyrinth from… you know, *Labyrinth*. Only instead of ghosts or goblins, there are *librarians*, which are far scarier."

"You know there's an actual haunted library in *Ghostbusters*, right?" Charles gave her a sideways glance.

"Yeah, in boy *Ghostbusters*," Alex waved her hand dismissively. "You know that movie is dead to me. Girl *Ghostbusters* is sooooo much better."

"Shut up," Charles scoffed. "You're just in love with Kate McKinnon."

"Uh, yeah!" Alex grinned. "Who *isn't* in love with Kate McKinnon? She's like, one of the top ten hottest women of all time."

"So any Kate McKinnons in your haunted library?" Charles asked, prompting Alex to break out in a wide grin.

"Actually, one of the librarians is *super* hot," said Alex. "But not in a Kate McKinnon sort of way, more like a Karen Gillian. She's even got an accent. It's hot AF."

"Ooh, a sexy librarian. Does she have glasses? I love a girl in glasses," Charles said, sounding so incredibly *gay* even as he tapped into his straight half.

"No, no glasses," Alex shook her head.

"Too bad. I don't know if she can qualify as an official 'sexy librarian' without glasses."

"Oh, she has plenty of... *qualifications*," Alex grinned. Just thinking about Cait made Alex get all warm and tingly. One upside to Jasmine's new 'open relationship' idea was that Alex didn't feel even the tiniest bit guilty for thinking lustful thoughts about her sexy new coworker. She still didn't like the idea of Jasmine seeing other people, and Alex wasn't ready to consider seeing other people herself, but she could at least let herself fantasize.

As Alex and Charles were loading their storage plunder into her car, Alex's phone buzzed with a chat message from Cait.

'Will you be coming soon?'

Alex stared at the message. It obviously wasn't meant as sexual innuendo, although that's where Alex's mind went first. *Coming where?*

'I'm sorry… What?' Alex messaged back. *Is that too informal?* Alex was hopeless with office formalities.

'We had a meeting scheduled for 1pm.'

"Oh, shit," Alex said under her breath. *That must be what I agreed to when I was too busy ogling her to pay attention.* "Well, that sucks."

"What's wrong?" Charles asked as he put the last monitor into the trunk of her little hatchback.

"I'm twenty minutes late for a meeting with the sexy librarian," Alex slapped her forehead. "So much for good first impressions."

'I am so sorry, I got wrapped up in something and completely forgot.' Alex messaged back.

'We can reschedule. I'll send you a calendar invite.'

'Ok, thanks. Sorry again!'

"I am such a fucking idiot," Alex groaned.

"Can't say that I disagree," Charles laughed at her.

"Shut up, Chuck," Alex grumbled. Charles glared at her, he hated being called 'Chuck.' He sighed.

"Well, it's been *super fun* spending my lunch break helping you," Charles said sarcastically; he fluttered his fingers at her in a faux-sweet farewell. "Bye, Lexie."

"Come on, where are you going?" Alex let the 'Lexie' thing slide since she had started the whole using-hated-nick-names thing.

"Hi-ho, hi-ho, it's off to work I go!" Charles sang. "Those tickets won't close themselves, you know!"

"You're not coming to help me unload?" Alex had taken for granted that he would.

"Nope, sorry," he shrugged as he walked backward away from her car and toward the student union. "Maybe ask your *sexy librarian* to help."

"Yeah, right," Alex rolled her eyes.

"It doesn't hurt to ask for help, *Lexie*." Charles maintained his sweet, sing-song voice.

"Bye, *Chuck.*"

Alex wasn't exactly the type to ask for help, and Charles knew that. She'd only asked him for help because they were tight. That's what friends did, it didn't mean Alex couldn't move the monitors herself. If she were to ask for help from some skirt-wearing librarian, Alex's ego wouldn't survive the humiliation.

Alex had grown up being the skinny little girl among her big, strong older brothers. She was still petite, scrawny even compared with big, blonde bi-boy Charles. If Alex didn't assert herself, she knew people would assume she was weak. A little girl, always in need of assistance. She felt like she'd spent her entire life proving people's first impressions wrong.

It wasn't all ego and posturing; Alex was pretty damn strong, and always had been. As a kid, she'd spent most of her waking hours up a tree or at the top of the playground. As an adult, she parlayed that aptitude into rock-climbing. She was a decent climber and had the muscles to prove it. *I don't need help carrying a little computer equipment.*

Alex slammed the trunk door shut, jumped into the driver's seat, and sped back to the library. She'd been late to her meeting with Nancy and then completely missed the one with Cait; that wasn't a good start. Geoff had sent her away to the library because he already didn't like her. If she fucked up there, she could be in real trouble. She did not want to lose her job. Even being stuck in the library was better than her last job - working at the computer store in the mall. That job had been truly soul-crushing. CUIT felt like heaven in comparison. *I guess the library isn't hell, just purgatory,* she reasoned. *It could be worse.*

As she drove back to the library, the dark gray sky lit up with lightning, and it started to rain.

"It's worse," she muttered. The rain went from a light sprinkling to torrential downpour as Alex unloaded her equipment. Alex was regretting just about every choice she'd made today as she ran back and forth from her car to the library.

"Oh, hello! You must be the new IT support!" A man standing beside the circulation desk greeted her as she hobbled through the entrance. He was short, with a generic white-man haircut, and a sweater vest that screamed 'forever single.' He looked at her appraisingly as he sipped tea from an oversized *Bookaholic* mug. *Oh god, don't offer to help,* Alex thought.

"Hi, yeah, I'm Alex," she said through clenched teeth as she struggled to carry two monitors at once through the stacks. The monitors weren't that heavy, but they were awkward as hell.

"Nice to meet you, Alex. I'm Manny, I'm one of the research librarians," he introduced himself as he followed her through the library. She couldn't help but notice that he *didn't* offer to help.

"Nice to, *oof*, meet you," Alex said as she almost ran into an awkwardly placed study table. Manny continued to trail along behind Alex, making inane small talk and loudly sipping his tea. Alex set down the monitors at her office door and went back for round two. Manny stayed on her heels like a stray puppy. He never shut up, except to drink tea, and he never offered to help. Four trips later, Alex's arms were numb with over-use, but everything had been moved.

"Well, I suppose I'll see you around! Toodles!" Manny wandered off the second Alex set down the last load. *What a weirdo.*

Alex stood in her office, not quite sure what to do next. She was soaked with rain and sweat. She peeled off her flannel shirt and set it on the radiator to dry. The navy-blue tank top she was wearing underneath wasn't exactly 'work attire,' but it didn't matter, she was alone in her office. *My very own office.* She got to work setting up her space.

Alex was on all fours under her desk, plugging things in when there was a light knock at the door. She jumped, startled, and hit her head. Pain shot through her skull.

"Ow, fuck," she muttered.

"Alex? May I come in?" a soft voice called in a maddeningly sexy accent. *Cait. Shit.*

"Yeah, just a second," Alex felt her face burn with embarrassment. She slowly backed out from under the desk on her hands and knees, hoping to god that she wasn't flashing Cait any butt-crack.

As Alex stood up, her eyes followed the length of Cait's legs, dressed today in tight black pants, up to her body covered in a loose-fitting cowl-neck sweater, and then to her face, framed by shiny copper hair. She was as gorgeous as Alex had remembered. *She is definitely a sexy librarian, glasses be damned.* Alex cleared her throat, awkwardly. *What I need to remember is to actually listen when she talks this time*, Alex told herself.

"Hey, Cait, sorry again about before, I really just totally spaced," Alex apologized. Cait didn't say anything - only stared, her perfect lips slightly parted. Alex looked down at herself. *Oh god, I must look like such a disaster.* Her hands and knees were dusty from crawling around on the floor, her hair was falling out of its ponytail, and she was standing there in a fucking tank top. *Real professional, Alexandria.*

"Sorry for my, uh, state," Alex stammered. "I had, uh, have a real shirt, but I was all hot and wet…" *Shit, that sounds dirty.* "From the rain! I don't usually take my shirt off at work." Alex laughed. Cait did not laugh. *I am a real picture of professionalism today, aren't I?* "Sorry, can I help you with something, Cait?"

"What now? Ah, no, not really," Cait blinked like she'd just woken up. "Sorry, I was walking by, and I thought I'd see if you'd got the invite I sent. I didn't mean to interrupt."

"Oh, no. No interruption. I was just setting up." Alex pointed vaguely back at her desk. "I have to go down there to turn them on." *What the hell is wrong with me?* "I mean put it in- er the plug. Plug the monitors in. That's why I was, you know, under the desk." *I should really just stop talking.*

"Did you then?" Cait asked.

"Plug them in? Well, not all of them…"

"Get my invite, I mean," Cait clarified, and Alex felt like even more of a moron, which a second ago she wouldn't have thought possible.

"Oh, yeah, that," Alex nodded. *Wait.* "Actually no, I haven't. But I haven't been on top of my email. Too busy-"

"Plugging things in, yes, I see that." Cait looked Alex up and down. "So, does tomorrow morning suit you for our meeting?"

"Sure, yeah," Alex nodded. *Damn, her accent is sexy. Wait, shit. What are we meeting about? Where are we meeting?* Alex hoped that information was in the invite sitting in her inbox because she did not feel like making any more of an ass of herself today by asking stupid questions to which she should already have known the answer. "I'll be there."

"Alright, well, see you then," Cait looked Alex over once more, gave her the barest hint of a smile, and walked out. Alex watched her go, enjoying the view of Cait's backside in those skin-tight pants. *Fuck... I really am all hot and wet.*

Alex considered the situation. It wasn't every day that a woman of Cait's caliber appeared in her life. The fact that meeting Cait had perfectly coincided with Jasmine's request for an open relationship could be a sign. Not that Alex really believed in signs. And yet the exquisiteness of this coincidence couldn't be denied.

'Are you really sure about this seeing other people thing?' she texted Jasmine.

'Yes. Why? Already have someone in mind?' Jasmine replied. Alex didn't know how to respond. Her mind flipped from lusting for librarian, to fear over losing her girlfriend in a microsecond. *What if she wasn't serious? What if this is some sort of test?* It wasn't worth the risk.

'Nope, just checking. I still only want you,' she responded. 'You available tonight btw?'

'No. I have a date with a woman from my gym tonight.'

Date? The word was like a blow to the gut. Alex dropped into her chair. *Fuck, that was fast. How long has she been planning this? Was she already seeing people before we talked last night?* Alex's eyes stung with tears.

All thoughts of Cait were forgotten as Alex pictured Jasmine in her tight yoga pants and halter top grinding on some hot yogi. Alex wiped her tears away with the back of her hand. *If this hurts so much, maybe*

I should just break up with her. But the thought of losing Jasmine entirely was even more painful.

"Alex?"

Alex looked up, startled. Nancy, the administrative assistant, was at the door.

"What can I help you with?" Alex asked, trying to hide her sniffles.

"Are you okay?" Nancy looked at her with concern.

"Yeah, just got some dust in my eyes," Alex lied.

"Are you sure?" Nancy asked. Alex nodded and wiped her eyes again.

"Yeah. I spent too much time fiddling with this dusty old equipment today. That's what I get for trying to pimp out my office on scraps." She smiled at Nancy. "What's up?"

"Can you help me with the printer? It's claiming to be jammed, but I can't find a jam," Nancy asked.

"Of course!" Alex said, cheerfully. "You know what a printer's favorite song is, right?" Alex didn't wait for an answer. "*We're jammin'*!" she began to sing, getting an appreciative smile out of Nancy.

Alex grabbed her damp shirt and pulled it on as she followed Nancy out of her office to the printer station.

"Jammin' till the jam is through…"

As Alex worked, she silently gave thanks for printers and their constant need for tech support. Fixing the issue was easy enough, but it still managed to take Alex's mind off the woes of her love life.

Chapter 4

With Jasmine out on a date tonight, Alex had no plans. But she knew she shouldn't sit at home alone. If Alex did that, she'd only spend the whole night obsessing. As soon as she got out of work, she called her former roommate and best friend in the whole wide world, Jenny Gu.

She and Jenny had met in college freshman year. They lived in the same dorm and had both been paired with absolute nightmare roommates. Alex and Jenny spent countless hours together in the dorm lounge, sexiled from their own rooms. During that time, they formed a special bond that nothing had been able to break since.

Jenny was a grad student at Cowling University. She was the reason Alex had applied to work at the university in the first place. They'd been roommates for their first year after starting at Cowling, but then Jenny met Markus and Alex was left to live alone. She'd never been mad at Jenny for that. Alex had expected to fill Jenny's space in the apartment with a girlfriend.

That hadn't panned out; 'cohabitation' wasn't something Jasmine was 'looking for.' Jasmine needed her space. She was an artist, so it made some sense. But all the same, Alex didn't like it. And now she couldn't help but wonder if Jasmine would have felt the need to see other people if they had been living together. *Now that she's dating, she's never going to want to 'cohabitate' with me.* That was a depressing thought. *I really hope Jenny's free tonight.*

"What's up?" Jenny asked by way of greeting when she answered the phone.

"I'm having a crap day. Hell, I'm having a crap *week*. Can I come over and vent?" Alex asked.

"Totally," Jenny agreed without hesitation. "You'll just have to put up with me doing my grading while you vent. I'm drowning in it. Have I mentioned that being a TA sucks ass?"

"Hmm, I don't know, that doesn't sound familiar," Alex teased. This was Jenny's second year TAing introductory-level courses for the math department. And from what Alex saw, Jenny was about ready to start beating the students with their own textbooks.

"Shut up and get over here. Markus is making stir-fry, and you don't want to miss it."

"An American boy making stir-fry for a Chinese girl? Shouldn't it be the other way around?" Alex joked.

"Fuck you. You know I can't cook."

"I do know that," said Alex with a smirk.

"Do you want my food and friendship or not?" Jenny asked in exaggerated exasperation.

"I'm coming, I'm coming!"

"That's-" Jenny began.

"What she said!" Alex cut her off with a laugh. "Jinx! See you in ten!"

Alex hung up the phone and turned on the car. She wondered, not for the first time, why she couldn't find a girlfriend that got her the way Jenny did. Why did she always have to fall in love with the beautiful yet difficult types like Jasmine? *Am I just a glutton for relationship pain? If that's the case,* Alex thought, *I need to find a new kink.*

When Alex arrived at Jenny's cozy little two-bedroom apartment, Jenny was sitting on the sofa, thumbing through papers.

"Hi, honey, I'm home," Alex called from the doorway. Jenny looked up, her shiny, chin-length hair falling forward over her face. She blew it out her eyes with a *foof.*

"Hey you, come on in!" Jenny beckoned. Alex kicked off her shoes and sauntered across the apartment. She was as comfortable here as she was in her own place. Alex greeted Jenny on her way to get a drink.

In the kitchen, Jenny's tall, dark, and supposedly handsome - if you were into the *male* thing - boyfriend Markus was putting the finishing touches on dinner. It smelled *amazing*, and Alex was instantly famished. As the three sat down to dinner, Alex filled Jenny and Markus in on the whole situation regarding Jasmine and their newly opened relationship.

"You should just break up with her if she's making you so unhappy," Jenny said.

"But I love her," Alex protested through a mouthful of Markus's surprisingly delicious stir fry.

"That's dumb." Jenny rolled her eyes.

"Love is dumb."

"You're dumb, Alex." Jenny shook her head. "You're holding on to a girlfriend who is literally out on a date with another woman. If Markus tried to pull that, I'd castrate him with these very chopsticks." Jenny jabbed at the air, violently with the wooden utensils. Across the table, Markus winced.

"Hey now, is that any way to say thank you for this lovely meal? Threatening a man's… manhood?" asked Markus.

"*Are* you seeing another woman?" Jenny raised an eyebrow at him.

"No…"

"Then I didn't really threaten you," Jenny stuck out her tongue. "It's more like a fair warning. Cheaters get chopstick castrations. No cheatin', no chopsticks. Easy-peasy, gonad squeezy!"

"Can we stop talking about my balls while we're having dinner with Alex?" Markus pleaded. "She's the one who has a cheater to castrate."

"Look, she's not cheating, and I'm not going to castrate her, or like hysterectomy her or whatever the girl version is," Alex insisted. "And I'm also not going to break up with her. So what do I do? I don't think coming over here to hide from my feelings every time she has a date is going to work as a long-term solution."

"Try dating other girls then," Jenny suggested. "Do what she wants you to. Maybe it'll make you feel better, and maybe it'll even show you how many people out there are better for you than High Queen Jasmine."

"Maybe..." Alex was far from being convinced, but she rolled the idea over in her mind once more. *At least thinking about finding a date might keep my mind off of whatever Jasmine is doing. Or whomever Jasmine is doing...*

"At the very least, you should keep your eyes open," Jenny said, waving her chopsticks at Alex like a teacher scolding a student. "There are other pretty lesbians out there, you know."

"And bi chicks!" Markus added as he began to bob to an imaginary beat. "Your girl just kissed a girl, *you* do bi chicks." He winked at her as he sang.

"Shut up, Markus," Jenny swatted at him. She turned back to Alex. "And I'm sure some of them are even decent human beings too," said Jenny sternly.

"I am keeping my eyes open," Alex insisted. "It's not like being with Jasmine made me stop noticing other women. Haven't I told you about Cait? The sexy librarian at work?"

"Um, no!" Jenny set down her chopsticks and picked up her wine. "You've got a thing for a librarian? Spill the tea, girl!"

"She's *gorgeous*," Alex sighed as she let visions of Cait fill her mind. "She's like right out of an old school pinup magazine, she's that level of hot. She's got the most amazing long red hair, perfectly curvy, with legs for days…" Alex sighed again.

"Nice tits?" Markus asked. Alex laughed.

"Oh yeah, she wears these sweaters that cling *just* right…" Alex felt a tingle between her legs as she conjured up images of Cait's round breasts, and she had to bite her lip to keep from sighing a third time.

"Okay, enough of that," Jenny scolded the two of them. "Do you like anything about her as a *person*?" Jenny prompted.

"I don't really know her yet," Alex said with a shrug. "She's a librarian. Her accent is just killer, though. I could listen to her talk for hours."

"I guess that's a start… Have you considered actually making a move on her? Now that you have this new-found freedom?" Jenny asked.

Alex shrugged. Of course, she had. It was one of the first thoughts to pass through Alex's mind once she'd gotten over the initial shock of the whole situation. But 'making a move' on Cait was easier said than done. Alex wasn't exactly a smooth-talking pick-up artist. She had very little faith in her ability to flirt. Her style was more along the veins of blatant *'hi, you're pretty'* awkwardness. And Alex wasn't even confident that Cait liked women. She got a vibe, but her 'gaydar' had failed her before - it was too easily thrown off by wishful thinking.

"We have a meeting tomorrow. Maybe I can try to flirt. A little," Alex said. "I doubt it will actually go anywhere, but I suppose I could use the practice…"

Alex wasn't even sure she'd want it to go anywhere. When Alex started thinking of really doing something with another woman, her mind quickly flipped to picturing Jasmine doing things with other women. Or other women doing things to her. And doing them better than Alex did. And that didn't do her confidence any favors. *It doesn't hurt to try. Cait is pretty, flirting could be fun. It's not like anything is going to come of it.*

Chapter 5

Alex gave herself extra time to hunt down Cait's office, so she'd be sure not to miss their second attempt at a meeting. She ended up being five minutes early, so like the awkward geek she was, she hid a couple of stacks away and played on her phone until the meeting time arrived.

"Cait?" Alex poked her head inside the door. Joan was sitting at a desk in the office, looking right at home. *Crap, crap, crap. Did I go to the wrong place?*

"Over here, Alex," Cait's unmistakable voice called from behind her. Cait was sitting on the other side of the room at her own desk. "Have you met Joan? We share an office," she explained like Alex was some kind of idiot. At least she felt like some kind of idiot.

"Oh, yeah, hi, Joan."

"Nice to see you again, Alex. Cait, do you need the room?" Joan asked.

"That shouldn't be necessary," Cait smiled and summoned Alex over to sit in a chair beside her desk. Cait was looking spectacular today, as always. She was wearing a skirt again. This one was shorter and showed off just about as much leg as possible in the workplace. It took significant effort not to stare at Cait's milk-white thighs or the hint of cleavage deep in the v-neck of her sweater. *Be professional*, Alex reminded herself. Flirting was one thing; ogling was another. Jenny would not approve of ogling. Nor would Jasmine. *Don't think about Jasmine.*

"Hey, Cait," Alex grinned at the pretty librarian. "Let's get this party started, eh?" Cait smiled faintly at her.

"How are you today, Alex?" Cait asked with that alluring rising inflection. She lightly brushed Alex's arm, sending a shiver down Alex's spine. "Settling in alright?"

"Yeah, I think so," said Alex. "Although I keep getting turned around. I swear the shelves move when I'm not looking, they're like those staircases at Hogwarts, you know, in *Harry Potter*."

Cait laughed a sweet bubbling giggle that made her face pink and her eyes crinkle adorably. Alex didn't know if Cait was laughing at her or with her, but she didn't care, she just liked the sound.

"I could use a Marauder's Map if you have one handy," Alex added with a grin.

"Only if you solemnly swear you are up to no good," Cait said, her voice low and teasing. Alex felt herself blush, and Cait giggled again. *Is she flirting with me?* It might just be the accent, it was hard to tell.

"Where are you from?" Alex asked, leaning in closer, her elbow on Cait's desk.

"Ireland."

"Where in Ireland?" Alex asked although she didn't know why she asked. The only Irish city Alex knew of was Dublin, and she didn't even know much about that. Geography was not her strongest subject.

"Trust me, you haven't heard of it," Cait said with another teasing smile. *She is flirting.*

"Well, your accent is really… nice." *Ugh, I bet Americans say that to her all the time, she has to be so sick of it.* But Cait didn't seem bothered. In fact, she laughed again.

"Could you tell that to my mum? She thinks I sound like a right *eejit* now that I've been living here in the States for so long," Cait said, her accent thickening slightly as if calling attention to it had reminded her how she was supposed to speak.

"Well, you sound *brilliant* to me," Alex said in her best British accent, which wasn't any good, but it was the closest thing she could do to imitating Cait.

"*Jaysus*, that was bad," Cait laughed again. "Don't quit your day job, Alex."

From across the room, Alex caught Joan glancing sideways at them, lips pinched in annoyance. Alex had almost forgotten she was there, caught up as she was in flirting with Cait. Alex cleared her throat.

"Speaking of my day job, I should probably get to it."

"Right." Cait sat up. "Let's talk about this system upgrade you've got planned. Do you have to do it with everyone?" Cait looked expectantly at Alex. '*Do it with everyone.*' The twelve-year-old boy inside Alex snorted with laughter. On the outside, Alex managed to calmly explain what she would need to do to each computer and how much time it would take per machine. It wasn't until she was almost done that she noticed Cait's apprehensive expression.

"Is there a problem?" Alex asked.

"You need to back-up every computer to 'the cloud,' you say? Before the upgrade?" Cait's eyes were narrow and uneasy as if Alex had suggested she cuddle a tarantula, not back-up some computers.

"Yeah…?"

"I'll have to meet with the senior library staff about that. Can I get back to you?" Cait asked.

"Well, I guess. But I have to do this migration, I can't *not* do it… it's just a matter of when." *And the sooner I do it, the sooner I'll have the chance to be unexiled.*

"CUIT cannot dictate our data policies," Cait said, her voice suddenly cool. *What's going on here?* Alex felt like she'd missed something.

"I'm just saying what I was told," Alex said with an apologetic shrug.

"Yes, well, apparently I wasn't told quite enough," Cait grumbled. Her expression grew distant as if lost in thought. Alex waited, unsure of what to say. *Didn't Geoff already arrange this project with the library staff? He already 'arranged' for me to work and extra thirty minutes a day. Didn't he tell them what I would be doing in all my copious time?*

"Is there a problem?" Alex asked. Cait blinked at Alex as her eyes refocused on the room around them.

"Perhaps." Cait pursed her lips. "Thank you, Alex. I'll get back to you once our staff has considered the situation."

"Uh, okay. Do you know when that'll be?" Alex asked.

"I can't promise we'll have a decision, but I'll make sure it's on the agenda for our next staff meeting." Cait's voice remained cool and detached.

"I have to give Geoff an update at my next check-in…" Alex fidgeted with her ponytail. She'd been so enamored with Cait's beauty she'd almost forgotten that Cait was a *librarian*. University librarians had a history of butting heads with the tech department. And if Geoff hadn't already cleared this project through them… Alex got an uneasy feeling in the pit of her stomach.

"Tell him that we're taking the matter under advisement," Cait said sharply.

"Okay, yeah, no problem," Alex tried to shake off her uneasy feeling. "I suppose a little delay won't be too bad. I've got other work to do. Just tell me once you've met… oh, would you want me to be there? To answer questions?"

"I don't think that will be necessary. If we have questions, I'll let you know," Cait said, turning to her computer. "Thank you, Alex."

Alex sat there awkwardly for a moment before she realized this was Cait's way of telling her to leave.

"Okay, I guess I'll see you around," Alex got to her feet and made for the door. "Talk to you later."

"See you around, Alex," Cait said, she glanced briefly up from her screen and smirked. "Don't get lost."

Alex replayed the exchange in her mind as she meandered her way back to her office. Something about the migration project had spooked Cait. Alex didn't know why. It was pretty standard stuff. *Why are librarians so weird?*

Chapter 6

To Alex's great surprise, Jasmine invited her over to her place for dinner. She even cooked. Jasmine was a fantastic chef. She hated culinary monotony and would try new things in the kitchen as often as time allowed. When Jasmine decided to try a new recipe, it was always a whole evening event. Tonight, it was vegan paella. Alex wasn't allowed to help, so she sat across the island countertop and sipped a beer while her girlfriend cooked.

As Jasmine measured and mixed, Alex let her eyes wander around the spacious loft apartment. Jasmine had several paintings leaning against the back wall that Alex hadn't seen before. *When was I last here?* It had been a while. One of the paintings showed the outline of a woman in blues and purples. *Did she invite the yoga girl over? Did she paint her?* It had been a long time since Jasmine had asked Alex to sit for her. She didn't like monotony in figure models either. *And apparently, she doesn't like monotony in girlfriends.*

"How was your *hot gym date*?" Alex asked, trying not to sound bitter.

"Oh, it was alright," Jasmine replied with a shrug. "Her name is Stella, by the way."

"Are you going to see her again?" Alex didn't know why she was asking. She couldn't help herself, some sick, masochistic part of herself had to know.

"I haven't decided yet. Stella isn't very bright, truth be told. But she's
fucking *hot* and *very* flexible…" Jasmine looked at Alex. "Do you really want to hear this?"

"No, not really," Alex said dully. Her stomach had turned the second Jasmine had called this other woman 'hot.' *Not just hot, 'fucking hot' and flexible. Goddamnit.* Her stomach lurched again, and Alex took a large gulp of beer. Jasmine walked around the countertop to kiss Alex on the cheek.

"I'm sorry, Lexie," she said before returning to her pots and pans. Alex hated when anybody else called her 'Lexie,' but somehow, when Jasmine said it, it made her feel special. And it cooled some of the jealousy.

"It's okay, I asked."

She's still my girlfriend. 'Stella' was just a stupid date. Jasmine and I have history. Alex went back to sipping her beer and gazing around the bright open apartment. She caught sight of Jasmine's teal bicycle.

"Hey, do you have an extra bike I could use?" Alex caught the look on Jasmine's face and hurried to amend her statement. "Not for going to and from work, just to go across campus. The parking around the library is such a nightmare, I figure it'll be easier to bike if I want to meet people from CUIT for like coffee or whatever."

"Yes, of course, I'll get one out of storage for you," Jasmine smiled. "Oh, Lexie, I'm so glad you're finally giving cycling a real chance. You've been so impossibly stubborn, I'd almost given up talking sense into you."

"I haven't joined your two-wheeled cult, I just need some simple transportation," Alex said with a sigh.

"That's the whole point, Alex. Simple, healthy, environmentally-friendly transportation," Jasmine said it with such self-satisfaction that Alex almost wished she'd asked somebody else. *Who else do I know who has like three extra bikes in storage?*

"Whatever." Alex drained her beer. "Is dinner ready? It smells amazing."

Jasmine's cooking was delicious as always; her vegan paella was better than it had any right to be. Alex ate as much as she dared. She wanted to get lucky tonight, and she did not want Jasmine to think she looked 'pregnant' this time. Alex did the dishes while Jasmine regaled her with the latest gossip from the local art community.

"I almost feel bad for Jorge," Jasmine sighed with exaggerated empathy. "He's been talking up his show for so long, it was sad how painfully *commercial* it turned out to be."

"Yeah, sucks to be Jorge," Alex agreed vaguely as she rinsed dish soap off a plate.

Jasmine wrapped her arms around Alex from behind, surprising her so much she almost dropped the plate. Jasmine kissed the back of Alex's neck, sending a warm tingle from the point of contact all the way down to her toes. She sighed.

"Are you done yet?" Jasmine asked in a throaty whisper that screamed *sex*.

"Yeah, just about." Alex shivered in anticipation as she rinsed the last glass and dried her hands. *I'm gonna bang my girlfriend...* Alex turned around and kissed Jasmine, lightly at first and then deeper, her tongue venturing out. Jasmine's tongue met hers as she kissed Alex back for a brief few seconds before turning her head away. *Playing hard to get?* Alex kissed along Jasmine's neck, breathing in the scent of jasmine and patchouli.

"Aren't you in the mood?" Alex asked in a low whisper.

"Mmmm, I might be," Jasmine teased.

"We'd better find out for sure."

Jasmine squealed as Alex picked her up and carried her over to the bed. Alex laid her down and climbed on top of her. She dug her fingers into Jasmine's hair and kissed her fiercely. Jasmine arched her back, pushing her hips hungrily against Alex. With her legs, Jasmine pulled one of Alex's thighs between her own and began to grind. Alex didn't let her get far before she pulled away. Jasmine whined, writhing in desperate desire. Encouraged, Alex tore off Jasmine's clothes before removing her own.

Kneeling on the bed, Alex looked down at Jasmine's naked body. Alex hardly knew where to begin. Her own arousal throbbed between her legs. Ignoring her own need for the time being, Alex ran a hand between Jasmine's breasts, along her abdomen, and down between her legs. Jasmine moaned and arched her back again, pushing herself against Alex's fingers. Alex dipped her fingers into Jasmine's wetness and spread it in small circles around Jasmine's clit. Jasmine laid with her head back, eyes closed, enjoying Alex's attention to her body. Jasmine came once as Alex fingered her, small shudders shaking her body. But she continued to moan encouragingly and buck against Alex's fingers, clearly wanting more. Alex couldn't help but notice that once again, Jasmine was making no attempt to return the favor.

Alex touched herself with her other hand. The pressure of her own fingers on her clit made her sigh. She was just as wet and ready as Jasmine. She looked down at her girlfriend. She was lying back, eyes closed in single-minded focus on her own pleasure. *I guess I'll have to be enough for both of us.* Alex pushed

Jasmine's legs further apart. Straddling her, Alex lowered herself down and pressed her clit against Jasmine's. *Oh, that's the spot.*

Jasmine moaned as Alex began to ride her. Jasmine shifted her hips in rhythm with Alex's motions, her moans rising in pitch until she cried out loudly and came again. She shuddered, arched her back, and screamed.

"Oh, fuck, my god!" Jasmine's body froze momentarily and then relaxed, satisfied. But Alex wasn't done, her heat and desire mixed with frustration. She wanted to fuck her girlfriend, *and* she wanted to get off doing it. Even if Jasmine wasn't going to do much to help. With one hand on Jasmine's right breast and the other gripping her thigh, Alex rolled her hips, grinding against Jasmine as she felt the heat build and build. *Come on, come on.* Her legs burned, sweat rolling down her back. Alex didn't slow until she felt the wave of orgasm wash over her. After it subsided, she collapsed, exhausted but satisfied, onto the bed next to Jasmine.

"That was fun," Alex said, breathlessly.

"Uh-huh," Jasmine agreed without much enthusiasm. She rolled over, reached for her phone, and began texting.

"What? Wasn't that good?" Alex asked.

"Yes, Alex, it was perfectly nice," Jasmine said, not looking up from her phone. *'Perfectly nice'*? Jasmine had seemed pretty enthusiastic while Alex was getting her off.

Alex watched Jasmine's face as she typed something out; she smiled as she read the response. It wasn't just any smile. It was a flirty smile, an I-like-you smile. And it wasn't for Alex. Alex's gut twisted.

"Who are you texting?" Alex asked.

"Shoshannah."

"Is that a woman you're seeing?" *Why am I asking when I don't want to know?*

"Uh-huh," Jasmine said absently. Alex frowned. Her post-coital bliss evaporated as quickly as water on Mars.

"Could you maybe *not* text with her while you're in bed with me?" Alex asked tersely. Jasmine rolled over to one shoulder. She looked Alex over as if deciding if Alex was worth her time.

"Fine, I'm sorry," Jasmine acquiesced, putting the phone away and curling up to Alex instead. "It's just a little 'new relationship energy.' But I'm here with you now. Come on, tell me what's going on in the world of Alex."

Alex forced herself to let go of her jealousy. She told Jasmine stories of getting lost in the stacks at work, and of the odd things librarians had said to her while she unjammed their printers and restarted their computers. Librarians were a quirky bunch. She was just getting into the latest information on the big migration project - or lack of information really - when she noticed that Jasmine had fallen soundly asleep. With a sigh, Alex kissed her forehead and went to sleep herself.

Chapter 7

There was no news from Cait or any other librarian regarding the migration project the whole next week. In fact, any time Alex brought it up, her questions were met with hostile glances and vague comments about 'invasive oversights.' There were clearly rumors circulating. The librarians were happy enough to have Alex solve their little technical troubles. Still, anytime the larger project - the real reason why Alex had been sent there - was mentioned, everybody suddenly got very us-versus-them, their manic friendliness fading into quiet distrust. It was as if in the librarians' minds, they were fighting some dystopian nightmare, and Alex represented Big Brother. It was so ludicrous.

Alex would have found the library's lack of cooperation amusing if it hadn't been her problem to deal with. When the time came for the next CUIT check-in meeting, Alex still didn't have any progress to share. *It'll be fine*, she told herself as she walked through the student union and into the technology offices. *It's not like we're in a huge rush.*

Although Alex had never been a fan of this particular meeting, on balance, she was happy to be there. It was good to be back in central CUIT. It was like coming home. She felt comfortable in the familiar conference room, surrounded by tech geeks.

Charles was thrilled to see her, of course. He filled her in on all the office gossip, including how Alex's old cube had been turned into a temporary work station for the work-study students, and how much he hated it.

"Oh my god, the students never shut up," Charles bemoaned to Alex as they settled into their seats. "I have learned so, so many things I never wanted to know. I mean, who discusses their periods at work?"

"Dude, girls discuss their periods wherever they go," Alex snorted. Alex didn't like the idea of other people in her cube, but she was relieved that they hadn't put a full-time employee there. And if it was bothering Charles, all the better. Alex wanted to be missed.

"Still, I don't need to know *anything* about student va-jay-jays, thank you very much," Charles whispered.

"It could be worse," Alex whispered back. "You could be me. Not only am I living out in purgatory, but ever since they found out about the migration, I'm like public enemy number one over there. Evil IT girl, out to steal all their library secrets."

"Why? Do they think we're trying to spy on them or something?" Charles scoffed. "They're not even interesting enough to *think* about, let alone spy on."

"I know, right?" Alex rolled her eyes dramatically.

The meeting got underway. Each sub-department gave progress reports, necessary or not, on various projects and problems they were dealing with. Geoff wasn't happy with Alex's lack-of-progress report. But luckily for Alex, he seemed more upset with the library than with her. He promised he would 'have words' with the library director and the appropriate VP if necessary. He seemed sure that once he did, Alex would be free to get started on the project.

Geoff spent the remainder of the meeting time - and then some - giving them all a rambling speech about being assertive and confident enough to 'bring the client along.' The decisions CUIT made were the right ones for the university, after all. There should be no reason to resist if the facts were properly presented. Alex tried not to roll her eyes throughout the *entire* speech.

"Alex," Geoff called her out just as the meeting was wrapping up. "I don't think it's really necessary for you to come all the way to the student union for this meeting. Going forward, it should be sufficient for you to join us remotely."

"Remotely?" Alex stared dumbly at him.

"Yes, Alex. Remotely. You can use video chat to join us from now on," Geoff said. "There's no use in wasting your time coming all the way over here, especially when you have so little to contribute to the meeting as a whole."

"Oh, okay." Alex quietly agreed.

"*Ouch*," Charles whispered to her. Alex scowled at Geoff's back as he turned to leave.

"Guh, I hate Geoff so much," Alex huffed under her breath. The check-in meeting had been her only excuse to visit CUIT. If she didn't get to attend in person, she'd never see her real coworkers. And she hated video-conferencing as a general rule. *I need to figure out another way to see Charles, or I am going to go insane out there in librarian-land.*

Alex returned to the library, feeling even worse about her current situation. But there was nothing to do but wait and try to stay busy with the little things.

A few days after the check-in meeting, Alex received a terse email from Cait, requesting to talk with her about the migration. From Cait's tone, Alex suspected that this was not going to be a light and cheerful we're-all-friends-now type meeting. *What the fuck did Geoff say to the library?* Whatever 'words' Geoff had with the library director, they must not have gone over well.

On the way to their meeting, Alex prepared herself for diplomacy. *Can I fix things if Geoff made them worse?* She wasn't sure, but she could try. Alex arrived at Cait's office exactly on time. She knocked softly on the open door as she tentatively entered the room.

"Uh, Cait, hey. You wanted to see me?" said Alex. There was an awkward silence. Cait's officemate Joan gave Cait a knowing look and excused herself, leaving them alone.

"Close the door, please, Alex," Cait said. Alex did as she was told before sitting down in the seat beside

Cait's desk. Alex should have been one-hundred percent focused on the matter at hand - this was an important meeting after all - but one look at Cait and Alex could barely remember her own name.

Oh my god, she's so fucking hot. Cait was wearing a light blue shirt-dress that was more shirt than dress. Seated at her desk chair, Cait's legs were exposed to her mid-thigh. Her every movement threatened to reveal more enticingly smooth skin. Alex could feel herself getting aroused. *Don't look at her legs. Try to focus.* Alex swallowed and forced her eyes to Cait's face.

"You wanted to see me?" Alex asked again.

"Yes. And I suspect you know why." Cait's accent gave her words a weight that made Alex feel like a schoolgirl called out in front of the class. *Don't get the answer wrong.*

"The migration?" Alex asked.

Cait nodded slowly and solemnly. This was all being taken very seriously. Alex tried to keep her expression blank, and her eyes focused on Cait's. *Just pretend you didn't see her thighs. The migration is important. More important than how soft her skin*

*probably is or how it would feel under your fingers...
or your tongue... Stop it.*

"You've put me in a difficult position, Alex," Cait said. "I don't want to stop you from doing your job, but I can't let you move ahead with staff computers until the library director has signed off."

"I didn't mean to put you in any position," Alex said, wincing at the way her words had come out. *Dirty.* "I'm sorry. But I really am in the same sort of position as you. If anything, I'm under you." Alex winced again. *Jesus, Alexandria.* "I mean. I don't have any power, really."

"Isn't there anything you can do to stop CUIT forcing this down our throats?" Cait asked. Cait was looking intently at Alex while absently running the end of her pen along her bottom lip.

"I can stall for a while…" Alex said absently. The motion of Cait's pen, drawing attention to her luscious, pink lips, was driving Alex crazy. *Did I even listen to what she said? Come on, focus!* Alex replayed Cait's last words in her mind. She blinked.

"Wait, you said 'staff computers.' Does that mean I could work on lab machines?" Alex asked.

"I suppose," Cait said, nodding slowly.

"It would be easier to stall on the staff computers if it looked like I was making progress somewhere," Alex explained. "That might get Geoff off my back for a bit. Would that get you off?" Alex felt her ears burn. *What the hell is wrong with me?* "I mean, would that, uh, work?" she rushed to correct herself.

"Yes, Alex. That would be grand," Cait said. She seemed at least somewhat relieved by this idea. A small smile played on her lips.

"Great," Alex sighed with relief. "I can get started right away if that's okay with you."

"Would you terribly mind waiting another day to get started?" Cait asked.

"Uh, that's fine, I guess." Alex shrugged. "I have other things to work on… But can I ask why?"

"I think I'd like to observe the process if you don't mind," Cait said, straightening in her chair. It took all of Alex's willpower not to stare at Cait's legs, where the hem of her dress had inched up along her thigh again.

"You want to watch me do the lab machines?" Alex asked. Cait nodded.

"I do. Although my primary job is student research, the computer labs here have been my responsibility. I'd feel better going forward if I understood what it is that you're doing." Cait leaned forward and put her hand on Alex's knee. The touch made Alex's heart race. Cait looked intently into Alex's face. "It's not that I don't trust you, Alex. I only want to understand. I hope that having me along isn't too much of an imposition."

"Oh, yeah, no, that's fine," Alex squeaked. Cait's face was so close that Alex could smell the light floral fragrance of her hair, see the flecks of gold in her green irises. *She's so beautiful.* Alex felt blood burn in her face, ears, and between her legs.

"Fantastic," Cait squeezed Alex's knee. "I appreciate it."

"Oh, yeah, for sure," Alex awkwardly rubbed the back of her neck and willed the blood in her body to start flowing normally again. "I probably need help finding the computers anyway. Everything here is so… disorienting."

"Ah, I would hate for you to lose your *orientation*," Cait smiled as she sat back; there was a hint of laughter in the way that the corners of her eyes crinkled. "I'll find a time tomorrow to come to your office. From there, we can go down to the lower level lab. It's almost always deserted this time in the semester. It would make a good place to start."

"Okay, please come whenever you want," Alex said, once again hyper-aware of her unintended double-entendre.

"I will." Cait's smile widened. *Did she notice the phrasing too? Is it possible she's noticed all the dirty things I've said unintentionally?*

"Uh, great. Cool." Alex smiled back.

"Thank you for being understanding, Alex," Cait said sweetly. She stood up, and Alex followed suit. To Alex's surprise, Cait gave her a brief but very close, tight hug. Alex could distinctly feel the pressure of Cait's chest against hers, Cait's breasts pressed against her own. Alex felt her cheeks burn again. *What was that? I didn't do that. That was her.*

"Yeah, no problem. It's all good," Alex stammered. Cait's demeanor had noticeably relaxed since the start of their meeting.

"You've been a very welcome surprise, Alex," Cait said. "I was so afraid CUIT would send us some antisocial computer geek, straight from his mum's basement."

"Yeah, not all us computer geeks live in our parents' basements, you know. I live in the attic," Alex said. Cait stared at her. Alex put up her hands. "Just kidding. That was a joke. Sorry, my sense of humor can catch people off-guard. I don't live with my parents. I haven't lived at home since college. I have an apartment. Where I live alone. I used to have a roommate, Jenny, but she moved in with her boyfriend."

Alex had no idea why she was suddenly telling Cait all of this. Something about the combination of Cait's short dress and that inexplicably tight hug had sent her awkward gene into turbo mode, leading to this mad bout of verbal diarrhea. *Shut up, Alex.*

"Alright, well, I'll see you tomorrow then," Cait brushed Alex's arm as she all but pushed her out of the office. The whole interaction was incredibly confusing. Alex needed to talk about it with somebody. Like, now.

'Hey, you got time for lunch today?' Alex messaged Charles. 'I figured out I have enough time to meet you if I bike and you meet me at the sandwich shop.'

'YOU are going to BIKE??' Charles messaged back. 'Have you been kidnapped? Do I need to call the authorities?'

'Shut up. Can you meet me or what?'

'Yeah, girl. See you at 12.'

Chapter 8

Alex sat down with Charles at one of the three tiny tables in the small, locally-owned sandwich shop. If Alex had been working in central CUIT, they would have brought their sandwiches back to eat in the department break room. But that would have meant traveling an extra few blocks away from the library, and Alex didn't need *that* much exercise. This was going to be a long lunch as it was.

"Can I ask you a weird question?" Alex began as she unwrapped her sandwich.

"Shoot."

"You know when somebody hugs you, like super tight in that specific way, and you can tell they're basically coping a feel of your boobs with their chest?" Alex asked.

"I'm insulted that you would think I would…" Charles took a big bite of pastrami on rye. "But yes," he continued, through a mouthful of food. "I know what you mean."

"I swear to god Cait did that today," Alex said.

"Get out of town." Charles didn't look like he believed her at all.

"No, really!" Alex insisted. "We had a super awkward talk about the stupid migration shit, she tells me she wants to watch me do it-"

"*Do it?*"

"The migration, you perv," Alex pursed her lips. "Then afterward she hugged me in a really… chest-forward way."

"Yeah, *I'm* the perv." Charles snorted. "Are you sure you're not imagining things?"

"I suppose I could be," Alex sighed. *Am I?* "She also touched my leg."

"Your leg?" Charles raised a blonde eyebrow.

"Well, my knee, but..." Alex felt herself blush.

"It seems like you're reading a lot into it." Charles took another large bite. "Objectively, what really happened?"

Alex shrugged. She thought back to the interaction; she could hardly be objective. Alex's mind immediately focused on the weight of Cait's hand on her leg. To how much she wanted to put her hand on Cait's. Alex could see Cait's dress, inching up over her thighs. She pictured how it would feel to slide her hands along those thighs, to push up that dress, to grab her by the ass and lift her right on to the desk…

"Earth to Alex," Charles laughed.

"Sorry," Alex felt her cheeks burn. "I can't think straight. Not that I ever think *straight*… but *s*he's so hot, it's distracting. When I'm around her, all I can think about is… you know."

"So, are you going to try and get with her or what then?" Charles asked.

"I don't even know how I would. I've been in monogamous-relationship-land for too long. I barely know how to flirt anymore. All my witticisms keep coming out like witless-icisms."

"Don't they always?" Charles teased.

"Shut up, Chuck," Alex flipped him off. "Flirting is so stupid anyway. Why can't it just work like in the movies?"

"What movies?" Charles arched an eyebrow at her.

"You know," Alex gestured vaguely. "Like when the IT tech comes in to 'hook-up your computer' and the next thing you know, you're doing it on the desk."

"Oh, so by movies, you mean *porn*," Charles laughed.

"That could be a regular movie..." Alex insisted. Charles laughed harder.

"If it were a real movie, it wouldn't just go from 'have you tried turning it off and on again?' to..." Charles threw back his head and fluttered his lashes. "'Oh god, you've turned *me* on!' There'd be more steps involved."

"Alright, Mr. Smarty-pants, so what are those steps? I need to know."

"Girl, you are asking the wrong person. If I knew those steps, why would I be so painfully single?" Charles let out a self-pitying groan. "Being bi, you'd think I'd get twice as much action, but every time I look up, I'm surrounded by straight guys and lesbians.

Boo... No offense." Charles looked at Alex appraisingly. "What is it about this librarian that's got you all hot and bothered anyway? I thought you hated librarians."

How could Alex describe Cait without confirming Charles' accusation by sounding like a total perv? The woman was like sex on a stick, and Alex's mind was in full-porno mode. *She has the most bitable lips, most kissable tits, and most wonderfully spreadable legs.* Just the thought of her, and it was monsoon season in Alex's pants.

"She's a sexy red-head. What more do you need to know?" she said, waving a hand dismissively.

"It just seems like there might be easier ways to get girls other than flirting over tech support. Not to mention all the added complications of the whole workplace romance thing..."

"It's not like I'm looking to *date* her. I'm still with Jasmine. I just figure, she wants us to see other people and there's this hot chick right in front of me..." Alex wanted to sound more chill about the whole thing than she felt. In reality, the thought of actually going for Cait was scary as hell.

"How are things with Jasmine?" Charles asked.

"It's so weird." Alex felt her posture slump and her chest ache as she thought of her girlfriend. One minute, Cait had Alex all 'hot and bothered' and then *bam*! Just the *thought* of Jasmine made her lovesick. It was all very confusing.

"Weird good or weird bad?" Charles asked.

"Just weird, weird. It seems good, but it feels bad." Alex shrugged. "I don't know, but I swear I've slept with her more times since we 'started seeing other people' than I did in the six months before that."

"Maybe she just needed to get her pump primed somewhere else, now you're reaping the benefit." Charles finished off the last of his sandwich. "That doesn't sound so bad to me."

"Well, I don't like it," Alex huffed. "I like being with her, but I hate knowing she'd just been with somebody else."

"Alright, so figure out those 'next steps' and get your own 'somebody else,'" Charles advised, absentmindedly twirling his fingers through his short blonde curls.

"That's easier said than done."

"I'm just saying, don't sit there being bitter that Jasmine's seeing other people, and you're just *watching* other people."

"You make me sound like a creeper." Alex protested. "I'm not 'watching' Cait. I'm just, you know, noticing her."

"And you think she's noticing you?"

"Uh, chest-hug-grope, hello!" Alex didn't know if the chest-hug really was what she thought it was. But at the very least, it meant Cait wasn't totally repulsed by her. It was a hug. None of the other librarians had hugged her for doing her job. "It seems worth at least trying…"

"Alright, then. So, what's your next move, IT girl?" Charles asked. Alex chewed on her lip as she thought.

"I dunno. Keep trying to flirt or whatever… We're meeting tomorrow so she can watch me migrate the basement lab machines..."

"Ohhh, computer migrations are sooo hot," Charles teased.

"Shut up." Alex swatted at his arm.

"Are you gonna show her how you put your *thumb drive* in the right *slot*?" Charles said in a low breathless tone.

"Oh my god." Alex looked at the ceiling.

"Maybe have her hold down your *control button* while you *mount her drive*." Charles made a low moaning sound. "Mmmm, nice *firmware*, baby."

"You have got to stop." Alex laughed.

"You're the one who wanted the next steps in the porn story, I'm just trying to help."

"I don't know why I tell you things," Alex said with a snort. She looked at her watch. "Aw shit, I have to get back to work. You don't even want to know how many printers they've had sitting around waiting for service."

"Yeah, you go. Service those librarians." Charles kissed the air and winked.

"Oh, for fuck's sake." Alex turned and walked for the door. "Bye, Chuck."

Chapter 9

Alex strolled into work the next day with a bit more enthusiasm. There was a spring in her step as she thought about the planned migration. Alex was both nervous and excited at the thought of Cait 'observing' her work. The technical process itself was fairly dull. When doing this sort of work, Alex usually spent a lot of time mindlessly spinning in her chair while she waited for things to load. Having somebody there with her would make the time go faster. If that someone was a pretty girl, all the better.

Alex heard a knock, and she looked up. Cait was at the door to her office. *Oh my god.* Cait was wearing a deep red sweater dress and knee-high leather boots. Alex immediately felt her own body react to the view. The dress somehow seemed even shorter than the one she'd worn yesterday. It clung to Cait's body and highlighted every curve. Her hips, her waist, her breasts… *I bet her ass looks amazing.*

"Are you ready to go down with me?" Cait asked in her irresistible Irish lilt. *Did she just ask if I want to go down on her?* Alex blinked at Cait stupidly.

"Down...?"

"To the computer lab?" Cait added.

"Oh, right, sorry," Alex practically jumped out of her chair. "Lead the way."

Cait flashed Alex a small, impish smile that left Alex wondering just how much of her attraction to Cait showed on her face. *Does she know I thought about going down on her? Can she tell how badly I want to see her ass in that dress? This could be a very long day if-*

All of Alex's thoughts vanished when Cait turned around. All but one: *Oh. My. God.* Cait's tight round ass looked absolutely delectable in the tight sweater dress. The way it moved under the soft knitted fabric as Cait walked was mesmerizing.

"Have you been to the lower levels before, Alex?" Cait asked, turning back to walk beside her. Alex tore her eyes away from Cait's backside just in time. She hoped so, anyway.

"No, I haven't," Alex replied.

"Ah, well, you'd better stick with me then," Cait said, looping her arm through Alex's. "If you think the stacks up here are confusing, you're in trouble. The ones on the lower lever are *murder*."

Alex was barely able to breathe through her nervous excitement as Cait led her down through the dimly lit archives, weaving around and through the stacks, until they came to a rectangular room with a projector screen at one end and about a dozen computers on tables around the periphery. Cait flipped on one of the two light banks.

"Here we are," she announced.

"Does anybody ever come down here?" Alex asked as she wandered through the room, turning on the machines.

"Yes, but it's on a reservation system," Cait explained, her eyes tracking Alex as she walked around the room. "If no faculty or staff have booked it for a class or a meeting, then it sits empty."

"Isn't that kind of a waste?" Alex sat down at one computer station, and Cait pulled up a chair next to her.

"We open labs like this up during finals, but otherwise, there just isn't that much demand. It's dead quiet down here most of the time." Cait was sitting so close to Alex that their knees were touching. Alex could feel her heart beating thunderously against her ribs.

"Well, then thanks for coming down here with me, I would have been lonely," Alex said, cautiously rubbing her knee ever so slightly against Cait's. Cait didn't pull away.

"I am truly curious to see what it is you're doing that's causing all the fuss," Cait said.

"It's really not that exciting." Alex pulled out her USB drive and got to work, walking Cait through the process. Cait asked a few questions, but there wasn't actually that much to it, and soon they moved on to chatting about life outside of work.

Cait was easy to talk to, and the time passed quickly. Cait wasn't just beautiful, Alex discovered. She was also smart and funny. And listening to her accent never got old.

Alex told Cait about her family, and Cait did the same. Cait was the younger of two children. Her parents still lived in Ireland, as did her older brother.

He lived 'just outside the pale' and had done well for himself in the recent tech boom.

"He's the poster child for success. Job, wife, children," Cait sighed. "My mum and dad are so proud of him. I'm the one who causes all the trouble. Running away to the states, refusing to find a *man* to marry…"

"Refusing to find a *man*?" Alex asked. *Is that her way of telling me she likes women?* But before Cait responded, the computer Alex was working on suddenly went dark. "What the fuck?" Alex looked at Cait. "Sorry, I mean, uh, what the heck...?"

"Never apologize to an Irish woman for swearing, Alex," she laughed. "Besides, this one's my fault. I think I may have accidentally kicked the cable out." Cait pointed under the desk. Sure enough, the computer's power cord was unplugged and dangling near the heel of Cait's boot. "Sorry about that."

"Oh, that's okay," Alex said. Without a second thought, she got down on all fours and crawled under the desk to plug it back in. Once under the desk, Alex found herself in extremely close proximity to Cait's legs in their tall boots and short, short dress. She glanced up toward Cait, but her face was obscured by the desk. From her vantage point under the desk, Alex could just about see up Cait's skirt. *Peeking up skirts is not cool or professional*, Alex reminded herself as she fidgeted with the computer cable. Just as she turned to crawl back out, Cait shifted in her chair. Alex sat frozen on her hands and knees, as Cait slowly uncrossed and crossed her legs. Alex's eyes went wide. *Holy shit, she is not wearing underpants.*

Alex quickly turned her head away and tried to catch her breath. She took a moment to give thanks that she was not a man, because had she been, there would have been no hiding the tent she'd be pitching right now. As it was, Alex was mildly concerned that she might soak right through her pants.

"It's turning on," Cait announced. *It sure is.*

"Uh, yeah, just a sec," Alex carefully crawled out from under the desk. Alex felt dizzy as she stood. All of the blood in her body had rushed to her crotch, with none left for her brain. She steadied herself on the desk and closed her eyes. When Alex got the nerve to open her eyes again and look at Cait, the librarian was staring thoughtfully at her phone. She typed something quickly and put the phone away.

"I'm sorry, Alex, but I have to run. Come by my office tomorrow, and I'll show you to where the other labs are." She stood and gave Alex another quick, tight hug. *Sploosh.*

"Okay, see you tomorrow," Alex managed in a squeak. As soon as Cait was out of sight, Alex collapsed into the chair with a sigh. *Holy fuck.* She squirmed in her seat. She was so turned on, it was ridiculous.

'Are you free tonight?' Alex texted Jasmine. *Is it wrong to rush to see Jasmine after getting turned on by Cait?* Alex wondered. She remembered what Charles had said, '*Maybe she just needed to get her pump primed somewhere else.*' *Is that what I'm doing now?*

If Alex saw Jasmine tonight, would she be able to stay focused on her? Or would thoughts of Cait linger? Was Jasmine thinking of other women when she and Alex were together? The idea cooled her overheated libido.

'Actually, never mind. I forgot I have plans with Jenny.' Alex texted again. It was a bald-faced lie, but Alex suddenly didn't feel ready to see her girlfriend.

'Too bad. I was keeping tonight open for you. But I can see Shoshannah, so it's fine.' Jasmine texted back. Alex grimaced. Why does she always have to tell me? I don't need to know.

'You free tonight?' Alex texted Jenny.

'No, sorry. Study group.' Jenny responded quickly.

'Ok, no worries ttyl.'

It looked like it was going to be another night of videogames alone. There were worse ways to pass the time. Like migrating computers alone in a dark basement lab. With a sigh, Alex packed away her phone and got back to work.

Chapter 10

When Alex made her way to Cait's office the next morning, Cait was waiting for her with a steaming mug of tea. Alex was too polite to tell Cait that she didn't drink tea, so she took the offered beverage with a polite 'thank you' and followed Cait out into the stacks once more. Cait's outfit was slightly more conservative today: a black A-line skirt and a stiff white button-up shirt. She was still sexy as hell; anything would be hot on her. *Or nothing at all.*

Cait showed Alex several more small computer labs that she could work on. She couldn't stay to watch today but thanked Alex for letting her tag along yesterday. Alex was disappointed to be losing her work companion and eye-candy; the day was going to drag on doing these mundane migrations alone. Yesterday afternoon's lot had taken an age, and she had more than twice the number of machines to touch today.

"Before you go," Alex said, stopping Cait just before she was out the door. "Could you, uh, give me directions towards the nearest ladies' room? I keep getting lost in the stacks." Alex rubbed the back of her neck and grimaced. It was a little embarrassing, continually needing to ask for directions. She'd been working there for over a month and yet could only consistently find one bathroom. And that bathroom was several floors away.

"I'll walk you there," Cait offered with a small smile.

"Okay."

"Although the closest one isn't really a 'ladies' room,'" Cait added. "It's one of those big 'gender-neutral' single-stall ones."

"That's fine," Alex said, not entirely sure why that was relevant but rolling with it.

"This way," Cait lightly brushed her arm as she led the way out of the lab and back into the maze of books. Alex tried not to stare at her ass the *entire* walk through the dim shelves, but it was hard. Her backside was so enticing. The way Cait's hips moved as she walked, making her ass pop from side to side. It almost felt like she was doing it on purpose.

"Here we are then," Cait said as they arrived at the bathroom door. She stepped aside, and Alex thanked her before shutting herself in the bathroom. She was surprised to find Cait still outside when she came out and even more surprised when Cait pushed her back into the bathroom, closing the door behind the two of them. Cait pulled her in by the back of her neck and kissed her. Alex nearly fainted from shock.

"What are…?" Alex gasped.

"Did I read this wrong?" Cait asked with a knowing smile. Instead of answering, Alex pushed her against the door and kissed her back fiercely. Every touch of Cait's lips was like a spark, setting Alex's body alight with desire. Cait's fingernails on Alex's back left a trail of fire up her spine. Alex was overwhelmed and over-excited. She grabbed at Cait like a horny teenager.

Alex felt Cait's mouth smile under hers as Alex unbuttoned her shirt. Cait wasn't wearing a bra. *Holy shit.* Alex could feel the rush of wetness between her legs as she took in the sight of Cait's round breasts and perfect pink nipples. She grabbed one breast, brushing Cait's nipple with her thumb.

"*Jaysus*," Cait moaned softly and pulled Alex in for another series of fiery kisses. Cait slid her hands under Alex's shirt, and Alex let her pull it over her head. She'd forgotten how good it felt to have somebody who wanted to undress her, Jasmine hadn't done that in ages. *Don't think about Jasmine*, Alex told herself. Cait's hands were warm as they slid under her bra, pulling it off.

Once Cait had relieved Alex of her shirt and bra, she pressed her body hard against Alex's. *She had been copping a feel with her hugs, I knew it*. Alex pushed up Cait's skirt. *No underwear again. Oh my god*. Alex ran her hands over Cait's smooth round ass. So much rounder and firmer than Jasmine's. *No, stop thinking about Jasmine*. Alex squeezed Cait's behind, and the Irish woman moaned encouragingly.

"Mmmm, I want you, Alex." Cait unbuttoned Alex's pants and began to slide her hand down between Alex's legs. The anticipation sent shivers through her body. *When was the last time Jasmine wanted to touch me like this?* Alex's heart suddenly began to ache.

"I'm sorry, I… I can't," Alex heard herself say. Her body throbbed in protest as she pulled away from Cait. "I'm sorry. I thought I could, but…" She felt herself tearing up and gritted her teeth against it. She re-buttoned her pants with shaking hands. "My girlfriend-"

"Girlfriend?" Cait pulled her shirt closed.

"It's not like that… This isn't… I'm not cheating," Alex rushed to say. "She's… we're 'ethically non-monogamous.' I'm sorry, I should have told you." Alex struggled to re-dress herself. There was a lump in her throat and unshed tears in her eyes. *What the fuck is wrong with me?* She had been eye-fucking Cait for weeks, and now that she'd had the chance to get with her for real, she couldn't?

"What do you mean by 'ethically non-monogamous'?" Cait asked as she calmly straightened her skirt.

"She's still my girlfriend, but she also sees other people," Alex explained, too embarrassed to look Cait in the eyes as she did.

"She sees other people? And sleeps with them, I presume?" Cait asked. Alex nodded. Cait was taking this all very well, Alex noticed. She seemed to care more about Alex's reasoning than about the fact that she'd just turned down her advances. Cait tilted her head. "And you don't want to 'see other people' yourself?"

"It's not that I don't want to. But… Apparently, I can't," Alex sniffed. "I wish I-" She half-laughed, half-cried. "Do you know how badly I would like to...? And how frustrating it is that having a girlfriend stops me? When she wouldn't even stop me herself?"

"Are you okay that she is sleeping with other women?" Cait asked curiously.

"I don't have much of a choice."

"It sounds like you're not okay with it at all. Are you?" Cait touched Alex's shoulder. Alex looked up at her. Cait's eyes were filled with genuine affection. Like she actually cared about how Alex felt. Like the reasons for her unhappiness mattered. It was touching, and it compelled Alex to speak honestly.

"No, I'm not," Alex admitted. It felt good to admit that out loud. Like a tiny weight was lifted from her chest.

"Then it's fucking ridiculous," Cait snorted. She leaned against the sink. "If you're not okay with it, then there isn't much 'ethical' about it, is there?"

"It's not her fault. I agreed to go along with it. She doesn't know how I feel..." Alex leaned against the counter next to Cait, shoulder-to-shoulder.

"I have a hard time believing that," Cait shook her head, making her ginger hair fall into her face. "I've only known you for a little while, Alex. But from what I can tell, you wear your heart on your sleeve. There's no way she doesn't know you're unhappy with the situation."

I wear my heart on my sleeve? Alex wondered what Cait had seen on her sleeve. *How well does she think she knows me?* She had read Alex's attraction clearly enough. *Am I really that transparent?* Suddenly Alex felt embarrassed and guilty for the way she had been ogling Cait for the past few weeks. Alex had acted blatantly interested in her coworker and then rejected her.

"I'm sorry for dragging you into this, Cait," Alex apologized.

"As I recall, I was the one who dragged you in here," Cait smiled at her. She was so maddeningly beautiful, her cheeks flushed, her lips full and so wonderfully kissable. Alex cursed her own stupid heart. If she could be like Jasmine... but no.

"Still, I'm sorry. I should have told you about Jasmine. I have to admit, I get a little stupid around you," said Alex.

"You're not stupid, Alex."

"I don't know. I can be pretty dumb. And being around you totally stalls my brain." Alex shook her head. "You're just so pretty and so cool-"

"Cool?" Cait laughed. "I don't think I've ever been accused of being 'cool' before." Cait laughed again.

"I mean it. If things were different, I would get with you in a New York minute," Alex said, nudging her shoulder against Cait's.

"Well, if that's the case, let me know if anything changes because I think you're pretty 'cool' yourself, Alexandria Rossi." Cait nudged her back.

"Thanks-" Alex blinked. "Wait. How did you know my full name?"

"I looked it up." Cait shrugged like it was no big deal. But it was a big deal. Alex had gone through significant effort to hide her full name. She hated it so very much.

"How? I totally scrubbed my full name from all of the university systems you could possibly have access to. It's as hard to find as my social security number."

Nobody at work knew her as Alexandria. And she'd wanted to keep it that way. *It doesn't quite sound so bad in Cait's accent...*

"I'm a research librarian. It's what I *do*." Cait looked around. "Along that vein, I think I should be getting back to it. Can't spend all day chatting in the jacks."

"Oh, yeah. Shit. I kind of almost forgot where we were." Alex shook her head and wiped away her last lingering tears. Cait opened the door a crack and peered out.

"All clear," she stepped out into the library. The lights in the stacks had timed out when they were in the 'jacks,' and the whole floor looked deserted.

"Oh man, I am so totally turned around right now," Alex said in a hushed tone. The library was deathly quiet, and Alex had to wonder if the door to the bathroom was sound-proof enough or if the whole floor had heard Cait's '*jaysus*.'

"Don't fret, I'll guide you through. Although I'm sure that if you stop staring at my arse and pay attention to where you're going, you might actually learn your way around." Cait's tone was light and teasing. Alex liked that.

"Aww. What fun would that be?" Alex smiled at Cait. Alex may not be able to actually do anything with Jasmine on her mind, but she still could enjoy the flirty banter. Cait grinned back at her.

"So when do I get my own fun then? You're the one who turned me down, Alex, but you're still eye-fucking the hell outta me with those sweet baby blues." Cait's eyes passed up and down Alex's body. "You're an attractive woman, Alex. You should show off a bit more."

"You're not going to catch me going commando in a skirt," Alex laughed.

"I guess it's back to kicking out computer plugs for me then."

"What?" Alex asked, not seeing the connection.

"How better to get a look at your sweet little arse? Besides, I like seeing you crawling around on all fours." Cait winked at her.

"You did that on purpose to get me to...?" Alex laughed. "You are trouble, aren't you?"

"I try my best."

Chapter 11

Things could easily have gotten awkward between Alex and Cait after their little 'meeting' in the bathroom. But Alex found that in some ways, she was now more relaxed around Cait. They continued their wanton flirting as they got to know each other better as coworkers and friends.

Being in the library wasn't so bad. Alex had Cait to talk to and a long list of computers to migrate, interrupted now and then by the need to fix a printer or answer some other technical question. Alex still missed CUIT and her coworkers there, but the pain of her banishment had been downgraded from mortal blow to simple flesh wound. It still hurt, but she'd survive. Unfortunately, attending the weekly check-in meeting via video chat felt like salt in that wound each and every week.

If Geoff had just let her continue to attend the check-in meetings in person, Alex might even be able to find some happiness in her new position. At least she'd still feel like a part of CUIT. But no. *Geoff couldn't leave me with one shred of CUIT-happiness, could he?*

"I finished all the lab computers," Alex reported to Geoff and the assembled CUIT support group at the next meeting. "Do you know how many computers are *squirreled* away in corners of this place? It's *nuts!*" Alex grinned as her coworkers chuckled.

"Thank you," Geoff said, unamused as always.

"Seriously though, there are so many 'fecking' computers over here. Cait swears they all get busy over finals but-"

"Alex," Geoff interrupted. "What progress have you made on staff machines?"

"I still haven't gotten the librarians to let me run the migration on staff machines but-"

"So, the only computers you have set to back-up are the ones that don't store any data?" Geoff's tone was condescending and almost sarcastic.

"Well, yeah, but they're also on the new system," Alex explained. "That means that it'll be tons easier to manage when-"

"I know how the new system works, thank you, Alex." Geoff cut her off. If Alex had been at the meeting in person, this is where she and Charles would have exchanged knowing looks, and Alex would be struggling not to laugh. Geoff didn't understand half of what went on in his department. And he certainly didn't understand much about how the new system worked. But Alex wasn't at the meeting. All she could do was continue to stare at the tiny pixelated Geoff as he glared at a tiny pixelated version of her.

"What is the issue with the library staff computers?" Geoff demanded.

"The librarians aren't comfortable with it, they haven't let me-"

"This is not an optional process, Alex," Geoff said, interrupting her yet again. "I don't know why you and your librarian friends seem to be under the impression that it is."

"Have you talked to the library director?" Alex asked. Cait said they couldn't move forward without the director's approval.

"I have spoken with the VP, we have the go-ahead. I hope you're not trying to tell me how to do my job, Alex." Geoff said with venom in his voice.

"I'm not, it's just the librarians say-" Alex stammered.

"These are *university* machines, managed by CUIT. There is a clear directive," Geoff growled. "Get it done, or I will send somebody out there who can. You have until the end of the semester."

"Okay, I will." Alex didn't know what else to say. Somehow being dressed down over a video call was even more embarrassing than being dressed down in person. She felt about as big as her icon on the screen. She shut off her camera and muted her mic. She only half-listened to the rest of the meeting. *What am I going to do?*

'Hey, do you have a few minutes to meet?' Alex messaged Cait.

'Sure. Would you like me to come down to your office?'

'That would be great.'

A few minutes later, Cait showed up in Alex's office, holding two steaming mugs of tea. She looked as spectacular as ever, in a pencil skirt and deep purple silk blouse that draped enticingly over her perky breasts. Alex tried not to stare too blatantly as she tried to figure out whether or not Cait was wearing a bra.

"What can I help you with?" Cait asked and handed one of the mugs of tea to Alex, who took it without hesitation. For some reason, she liked the tea that Cait always brought her. It was interesting because all the tea Jasmine had made her try tasted like dirty hot water. And generally speaking, Jasmine had a wonderful sense of flavor.

Alex sipped her tea as she told Cait about the disastrous check-in meeting. Alex explained how she thought her best chance to make progress at this point was to meet with the director of university libraries, Mandy Walker. Alex thought that talking to the director might shed light on something that would help her find a compromise, a solution that could satisfy both parties. After the severe scolding from Geoff, Alex needed to do *something*. This was the only thing she could think of, and she was prepared to beg for Cait's help making it happen. But Cait jumped to offer her assistance right away.

"I know Mandy well, we have a good working relationship. I'm sure I could get you a meeting with her as soon as next week," Cait said.

"That would be great, thank you." Alex felt a little relief at knowing she was doing something to move the project ahead.

"You're welcome, Alex." Cait sipped her tea. "Would you like me to go with you to the meeting? Be a friendly face in the room?"

"Yes, that would be great," Alex looked sideways at Cait. "Why, though? Is Mandy unfriendly?"

"Oh no, nothing like that. She can be intimidating, but she's very kind," Cait assured her. "Don't worry, it'll be grand."

"Okay, cool. I trust you."

"I'm glad of that. I should get on to my research, I have a medieval history class coming in next week, and I still have a ton left to do," Cait said. She stood up and stretched. Alex felt a shiver of attraction run through her body as she watched Cait pulling her shoulders back and rolling her neck. *Holy hell, she's sexy. It's not even fair how hot she is.*

"Oh, and Alex," Cait relaxed her shoulders and gave Alex a knowing look. "The answer, by the by, is no. I'm not wearing a bra."

"What?" Alex stared at her. "How did you...?"

Cait threw her head back and laughed. "You're a bit thick sometimes, Alex," Cait shook her head. "I'll see you around." Chuckling softly to herself, Cait walked out of Alex's office, leaving Alex blushing furiously and grinning like a maniac.

A week later, she and Cait sat in matching carved wood chairs across a large desk from Mandy, the library director. Mandy was a stern-looking woman with dark hair pinned in a tight bun and deep frown creases between her thick brows. She was sitting up stick-straight and watched Alex enter the room with suspicious, hawk-like eyes. Mandy looked like she was made to be an old-fashioned one-room school teacher - ready to smack somebody with a ruler. Alex hoped that somebody wasn't her. *Don't hit the messenger, please,* she silently begged.

"You know, there are university IT departments out there who *collaborate* with their libraries rather than try to bulldoze them," Mandy said sourly. "I've seen IT and library work side by side. What CUIT is doing is highly irregular."

"I get that, and I'm sorry," Alex began.

"Alex really is here to help us figure this out," Cait added with a smile at Alex.

"CUIT doesn't even know I'm meeting with you actually," Alex admitted. "But Cait and I are kind of stuck in the middle, and we're stalled on what we can do on our own. I thought it might be worth trying to get a better sense of what exactly you don't like, so I can see if there are any technical loop-holes or compromises that will let us do the migration without… bulldozing you."

"Thank you, Alex. I appreciate what you're trying to do." The library director went on to describe their concerns regarding data privacy and legacy systems. "I've said as much to your director, you know."

"Yeah, but Geoff doesn't actually know anything," Alex said. The look on Mandy's face told Alex she'd been overly blunt, as usual. *Be professional.* "I mean, he's not as familiar with the technology as I am. I think there might be some middle ground here that he overlooked. I have to check on a few things, but I have an idea. I'll get back to you as soon as I can."

"Thank you, I look forward to hearing from you." Mandy smiled, and some of the schoolmarm harshness faded from her face. "It's been refreshing to talk to somebody from CUIT who knows how to listen for once."

Alex and Cait thanked Mandy for her time, stood, and walked out of the office together. Outside, the air was crisp and fresh. Fall was fading into winter, but with the sun shining brightly in the sky, it was perfectly pleasant weather for a walk. Red, brown, and gold leaves littered the sidewalks. Cait looked warm and lovely bundled up in her coat and scarf, her hair blowing in the light breeze.

"Do you really have an idea you think will work?" Cait asked as they walked across campus back toward their little remote library.

"Yeah, I do."

Alex explained the concept to Cait, not sure how much she'd be able to follow. Cait was quite intelligent, but she was a *librarian*. Cait seemed to understand more than Alex had anticipated because when Alex got to the key component - the element that made backup and migration possible without 'cloud' back-up - Cait stopped in her tracks.

"Alex, that's deadly!" she exclaimed. *She understands this project better than Geoff.* Alex grinned as Cait threw her arms around her and hugged her. It wasn't a chest-feeling, think-about-sex hug; it was warm and friendly. Alex liked it.

"Thanks," Alex blushed. "But let's not get too excited yet. "I'll have to look into a few things first. I need to be sure that specific solution with work with this specific system."

"But you think it will?"

"Yeah, I do."

"Then we need to celebrate," Cait said, her eyes shining bright moss-green in the afternoon light. Alex usually only saw Cait within the dim confines of the library. Outside in the sunshine, Cait was even more radiant. Her smiling was dazzlingly white, her cheeks flush pink in the autumn air, and her copper hair shone like a newly minted penny. Cait beamed at Alex, and Alex felt that indescribable pull to kiss her. But Alex knew in her heart that kissing Cait would mean giving up on Jasmine. And she wasn't ready for that.

"Okay, how do we celebrate? A pint down at the pub?" Alex said in a terrible imitation of Cait's accent.

"Not all Irish spend all our free time 'down at the pub,' mind," Cait admonished with a snicker.

"Okay, so what did you have in mind?"

"Ah, well, there is that library happy hour tomorrow…" Cait began. Alex burst out laughing.

"Okay, so drinking is still central to the plan, just not 'down at the pub'?" she snorted.

"Feck off," Cait pushed her playfully. "What do you know about going down to the pub anyhow, Alexandria Rossi?"

Alex gave Cait her very best you're-going-to-regret-asking face and cleared her throat.

"I've been the wild rover for many a year, and I've spent all my money on whiskey and beer!" Alex sang at the top of her lungs. *"But now I'm returning with gold in great store and I never will play the wild rover no more. And it's no, nay, never."* She clapped loudly. *"No, nay, never no more! Will I play the wild rover? No, never no more!"*

Cait laughed so hard tears were visible at the corners of her eyes.

"Stop, please," Cait begged through her laughter. Alex grinned and obliged. Cait wiped tears from her eyes as she tried to stifle her giggles. "How do you know that song?" she asked.

"A few drops of Irish blood runs through me veins, did I not tell ye?" Alex leaned hard into her put-on Irish accent.

"*Jaysus*. You have to stop," Cait shook her head, her eyes still bright with laughter.

"Or what?"

"Or I'll start talking in an American accent," Cait said, in one of the most god-awful American accents Alex had ever heard. Alex doubled over laughing again. Encouraged, Cait began to sing '*Take Me Home, Country Roads*.' Students passing by gave the two odd looks as they lost themselves in fits of giggles. Alex couldn't remember the last time she'd laughed so hard. It wasn't even all that funny, but there was something about Cait that brought out the giggling girl inside of her.

"Well, are you coming to the library happy hour tomorrow then?" Cait asked when they'd both caught their breath.

"I don't know..." Alex shook her head.

"Oh, come on. Why the hell not?" Cait asked.

"Well, as a personal rule, I don't stay at work after hours…"

"Trust me, it doesn't feel like work once we open the wine," Cait assured her.

"I don't know if I feel safe in that library after you open the wine," Alex snorted.

"Why's that?" Cait asked curiously, raising an eyebrow at her.

"Drunk librarians? Scary stuff." Alex said with an exaggerated shudder. "But mostly it's because I have a big mouth without the lubrication of alcohol. I'd probably end up actually calling Manny 'man-brarian' to his face or something."

"I'm sure he's been called worse. Have you seen how he dresses?" Cait nudged Alex playfully. "Come on, come to the happy hour. At least for one drink."

"Are you just trying to get me drunk to get me in 'the jacks' with you again?" Alex teased.

"Did you rid yourself of that girlfriend of yours?" Cait pursed her lips and looked at Alex like she was really thinking about it. Alex felt herself blush. She looked at the ground and kicked at a pebble on the sidewalk.

"Naw, I'm still with her. I'm seeing her tonight, actually."

"Ah, well, then don't worry about me, Alex," Cait said. "You won't find me giving you the ride knowing how you feel about your lady. If I had you, I think I'd want you all to myself anyhow."

Alex looked up at Cait. Cait looked away, and Alex thought she saw the pale woman blush. Although it could have been the cold air that put the pink in Cait's cheeks. *Is she teasing me? Or would she really want to date me if it weren't for Jasmine?*

"Alright, well, that eliminates that concern," Alex laughed awkwardly then sighed. "Still, I doubt I'll make it to the happy hour."

"Alex," Cait began.

"But I won't rule it out entirely." Alex held open the library door and followed Cait through. Cait's perfect lips twisted into a wry smile.

"That's better than nothing, I suppose… *Jaysus,* it's dark in here!" Cait squinted and rubbed her eyes, Alex did the same.

"Seriously. I feel like I just went blind," Alex said, blinking until the vague shape of the circulation desk slowly faded into detail.

"Do you need help navigating the stacks in your disadvantaged state?" Cait offered.

"Naw, I think I've got it. But thanks for all your help today, setting up that meeting with Mandy and vouching for me and all. I think we really have a chance at solving this thing. You're awesome, you know that?"

"Well, I'm alright. For a librarian." Cait winked at Alex and walked off toward her office.

Chapter 12

Alex excitedly told Jasmine about all the drama unfolding at work. Unfortunately, instead of focusing on the potential of Alex's new idea, all Jasmine seemed to zero-in on was her continuing confrontations with Geoff.

"Being loud and blunt isn't the same thing as being assertive. Are you actually affecting change, or are you just the loudest one complaining about the status quo?" Jasmine asked, her tone dismissive as if she already knew the answer.

"I'm helping find a solution," Alex replied. *Jasmine probably just didn't understand the technical aspects. She's not being hurtful on purpose.*

"If you say so," Jasmine rolled her eyes. Alex scowled at her, and Jasmine rolled her eyes again. "I'm sorry. You've just never been a very career-driven person, Alex. Although it sounds like you're determined to drive this job into the ground."

"If Geoff can't handle my brilliance, that's his loss," Alex said flippantly. She didn't want to give away how much Jasmine's words stung. "Speaking of *brilliance*, how's your new show shaping up?" Alex asked before Jasmine could respond; the topic of her own job had lost its appeal. Luckily Jasmine was happy enough to switch subjects and step into the spotlight. She filled Alex in on all the latest news from the studio.

Alex listened as attentively as she could, but her mind kept drifting back to work, her plan, and *Cait*. If somebody had asked Alex a month ago whether she'd ever find her place in the little library, Alex would have said no. Then it had happened without her even realizing it. She made a friend; she got comfortable among the stacks. She didn't feel the need to run back to CUIT every chance she got. She didn't even message Charles as often as she used to. *When's the last time I talked to Charles?* It had been a while.

"Alex, are you even listening to me?" Jasmine asked, hand on her hip, bright red lips pursed in irritation.

"Sorry, my mind wandered," Alex admitted.

Jasmine let out a long why-do-I-put-up-with-you sigh.

"See, this is what I like about Shoshannah," Jasmine's eyes flitted upwards. She smiled dreamily. "Shoshannah is so *creative*. She understands my world. It's so good to have that."

Ouch. Alex tried not to physically wince. *Why should that even bother me?* It was objectively true. While Alex did appreciate art and honestly enjoyed going to Jasmine's shows, she wasn't an artist. She didn't *get* art in the way that her girlfriend did. She was just a tech geek with a bachelor's degree in *geology* of all things.

"So good to hear about your *lovers*. Is this Shoshannah an artist?" Alex asked lightly.

"Actually, I've been meaning to bring her up," Jasmine continued. "I know you usually don't want to hear about my other *partners*, but Shoshannah and I have been dating for a while now, and I'd really love for the two of you to meet."

"What?" Alex blinked at her. *She can't be serious.*

"Think of it like a double-date," Jasmine said casually as if this were a totally normal thing to ask.

"Double-date implies two couples. That only really works if there are two of you," Alex pointed out. She squinted at Jasmine. "Do you have a clone I don't know about?"

"Don't try to be cute," Jasmine said tartly.

"I don't need to try, I *am* cute," Alex grinned and tried to pull Jasmine in for a kiss, but Jasmine pulled away.

"I'm serious. We're all going out to dinner together tomorrow," Jasmine crossed her arms and gave Alex one of her stubborn, chin-lifting pouts.

"What if I had plans tomorrow?" Alex protested. She thought back to the library happy hour. She hadn't really *planned* to go, but she didn't like being told she couldn't either.

"Did you have plans, Lexie?" Jasmine asked with a condescending lift in her voice. This time, being called 'Lexie' didn't feel so special.

"Sorta," Alex huffed.

"Oh, really? What plans? I thought Jenny was out of town this week."

"I have other friends, you know." Alex didn't want to sound defensive. Jasmine was right, she rarely spent time with people other than Jasmine or Jenny. Alex dealt with people all day at work; she didn't feel she needed a big social life outside of that. But that wasn't the point. "And technically we are non-monogamous," Alex pointed out. "I could have a date. You don't know."

"Do you?" Jasmine looked at her blandly - as if the idea of Alex having a date was so unlikely Jasmine couldn't even be bothered to waste a facial expression on the thought.

"No," Alex admitted.

"Okay, *with whom* do you have *plans*?" Jasmine batted her eyes impatiently.

"It's not like, *with* anybody, there's just this happy hour at the library…" Alex gestured vaguely.

"It's a work thing?" Jasmine sighed. "Do you have to go?"

"It's not like it's required," said Alex. "But-"

"But you *want* to go? To a happy hour in the *library*?" Jasmine didn't sound like she believed it. It wasn't the sort of thing Alex would typically choose to do.

"I told Cait I would," Alex heard herself say. It wasn't too far from the truth. She had discussed it with Cait. She knew Cait would be there and wanted Alex to be there also. Alex didn't really *want* to go. She barely knew anybody in the library, aside from Cait. And everybody knew Cait. Alex worried she'd end up feeling like an awkward groupie if she just followed Cait around all night. But even that sounded better than meeting this Shoshannah chick. "Yeah. I'm going to the happy hour. Sorry. Maybe another day."

Jasmine rolled her eyes to the ceiling and let out another exasperated sigh.

"Okay, *fine*, but can you meet up with us after? It's just happy hour, right? That can't go too late," Jasmine reasoned. Alex couldn't really argue with Jasmine's logic, as much as she wanted to.

"Sure, I guess," Alex begrudgingly agreed. Jasmine smiled and threw her arms around her excitedly. Usually, making Jasmine happy gave Alex some joy in return, but this did not. She felt trapped. *Great, happy hour with a bunch of librarians. Right before I go meet my girlfriend and her new 'partner.' Fucking fantastic.* Alex sighed. *Cait had better not have been joking about the wine.*

Chapter 13

Cait hadn't been joking about the wine. Nor had she exaggerated its effect on the library staff. The moment the first cork was popped, everybody seemed to relax into friendly, chill smiles. No more manic false cheerfulness *or* dirty looks. *Maybe librarians are just ordinary people, after all.* Even though Cait wasn't there when Alex first arrived, it really wasn't all that bad. Joan beckoned Alex in with kind words of welcome, and Alex sipped her wine as she listened to Joan and Trisha discuss fantasy football, of all things. After a few minutes, Alex excused herself to wander about the room.

The happy hour wasn't held in the depressing break room, as Alex had feared, but in the spacious 'reading room.' The space was furnished comfortably with an eclectic mix of chairs and couches that neither matched nor clashed. The walls were covered in beautiful wooden shelves filled with books - all fiction by the look of it. Alex walked around the room, glancing at the mix of titles.

"Can I help you find something, miss?" Cait appeared at Alex's shoulder.

"Just browsing," Alex grinned as she turned. Cait was wearing a soft grey sweater and had her hair pulled up into a loose bun. Alex couldn't recall seeing her with her hair up before. It was pretty. Cait was always pretty, but having her hair up softened her look from sex-bomb hot to cuddle-me cute. Alex liked it.

"Do you like to read, Alex? I realize I've never asked you that before."

"Oh, yeah, I love reading."

"What do you love to read?" Cait asked. Alex shrugged and turned back to the shelves of books. She let her eyes wander along their spines.

"Just, you know, fiction… sci-fi mostly. Nothing deep or anything." Alex felt her cheeks warm.

"Why do you seem embarrassed?" Cait asked.

"Oh, Jasmine always says I'm shallow, just looking for easy entertainment…" Alex shrugged. "She thinks it's a waste of time and brain cells to just read to be entertained and not *enriched*. She likens it to buying 'art' at Ikea. Like it doesn't really count."

"Your girlfriend is an *eejit*," Cait shook her head disapprovingly. "Books are entertainment. Trust me, I'm a librarian. Besides, I'm a murder mystery addict myself."

"I love the way you say '*murder*,'" Alex said, trying and failing to reproduce the word the way Cait did.

"You're so cute it kills me, Alex." Cait laughed.

"Would you say I'm *murdering* you with my charm?" Alex waggled her eyebrows suggestively. Cait laughed.

"Well, listening to your jokes is murder," she teased. "Don't quit your day job."

"I've heard that before," Alex laughed. She thought about her 'day job' and what Jasmine had said about driving it into the ground, and her smile grew sardonic. "You know, at this rate, I might not have the chance to quit. If this idea doesn't work, I'm gonna get my ass fired."

"I hate to see you so wrecked over how your boss is treating you," Cait said with a shake of her head. *Have I been acting 'wrecked'?* Alex wondered. She had been pissed about being banished to the library, then frustrated by the project. And the dressing-down she'd gotten in the check-in meeting had sucked the big one. It all bothered her, but was she 'wrecked'? Alex didn't think she let her feelings show that much. She waved her hand dismissively.

"It's okay. Geoff's a tool. But if this goes well, maybe he'll finally realize I'm not an '*eejit*' and let me back into central CUIT." Alex barely dared hope.

"You want to go back?" Cait sounded surprised.

"Of course, all my friends are over there. It's so much better," Alex stopped. The way Cait was looking at her made her realize she sounded like an asshole. "I mean, sorry, no offense."

"Only some taken," Cait smirked. "Can I get you another glass of wine?"

"I'd like that, although maybe I shouldn't… I have to go meet my girlfriend and her *lover* soon." Alex groaned. "God, I don't want to."

"Why don't you have another glass and tell me about that," Cait said, and Alex agreed. She and Cait took their wine and sat down on a deep brown couch in the corner of the reading room.

"So tell me about your girlfriend and her 'lover.' What's the story?" Cait sipped her wine and waited for Alex to explain. Alex didn't know why she'd brought it up in the first place. Maybe the magic of the wine had relaxed her a bit too much. But now, with the way that Cait was looking at her, Alex felt compelled to share.

"Remember how Jasmine's 'ethically non-monogamous'?" Alex asked. Cait nodded. "Well, she wants me to meet her new 'partner' tonight. *Shoshannah.*" Alex made a sour face and stuck out her tongue.

"You can't be comfortable with that," Cait looked at her curiously. Alex shrugged.

"It's important to her. So, whatever." Alex drank her wine and tried to control her obvious distaste for the whole thing.

"Does she know how you feel?" Cait was still looking at Alex like she was some sort of puzzle that needed solving.

"Naw, I doubt it." Alex shrugged again.

"Does she know you at all?" Cait shook her head. *Sometimes I wonder if she does.* Alex bit her tongue. She'd spent enough time for one night airing her dirty laundry.

"What about you, Cait? You seeing anyone?" Alex tried to shift topics.

"Not at the moment, although hearing about this Jasmine woman has me remembering all the reasons I'm glad not to be in a relationship. My last one was such a train wreck."

"Oh?" Alex looked at her questioningly, expecting her to go on. But Cait shook her head.

"I don't discuss things that are over and done with, as a general rule," Cait said. "I'm glad you broke your rule about stay late after work. It's been nice chatting with you, Alex."

"Yeah. This was fun, thanks for insisting I come…" Alex glanced at her watch. "Crap, I should really get going. We're still meeting about the test migration tomorrow, right?"

"Yes, nine o'clock." Cait nodded.

"Great, cool." Alex stood. "I'll see you tomorrow, Cait."

"See you tomorrow, Alex."

Chapter 14

When Alex arrived at the restaurant, Jasmine and a woman - presumably Shoshannah - were cozied up next to one another in a booth. It was a surreal experience for Alex, seeing her girlfriend and another woman, so obviously on a date, so obviously into each other. Shoshannah was cute enough. She had tight blonde curls and a plain face with a blotchy pink complexion that hinted at a history of acne. She was taller than Jasmine with broad shoulders. Alex wouldn't have been surprised if she'd played basketball or volleyball. She looked strong. Jasmine probably liked that; she loved being literally swept off her feet. Alex did not like the thought of Shoshannah carrying her girlfriend to bed. Alex immediately decided that she did not like Shoshannah at all.

Alex should have taken a moment to breathe, maybe even left entirely, but the three glasses of wine she'd had at the library happy hour had dulled whatever common sense might have possessed. So instead, Alex strutted over to the table, trying to project a sense of calm self-assurance. *I had her first. She loves me*, she reminded herself.

"So, you must be Shoshannah," Alex said, sliding into the seat across from them. "I'm Alex. Whatever she's told you about me, it's not true. Unless she told you I'm an *amazing* lover, in which case, guilty as charged." Alex grinned.

"Alex, really," Jasmine sighed. "Do you always have to be so much?"

"You know you *love* me," Alex sat back, hoping that her faux-confidence bolstered by wine would morph into some actual confidence.

"Don't worry, Shoshannah, she's not always like this," Jasmine said, giving Alex a cold look.

"It's nice to meet you," Shoshannah reached an awkward hand across the table, and Alex shook it. Shoshannah's hand was soft, and her handshake weak. *Maybe she's not as strong as she looks*. Alex smirked to herself.

"We already ate, I'm sorry, I didn't know how long you would be, and the drinks were just going straight to my head," Jasmine said with a flirty smile for Shoshannah. She didn't sound at all sorry. Alex brushed it off.

"No problem, I had some food at the happy hour. It was quite the shindig. Librarians really know how to party. In a quiet stand-around-and-drink sort of way. Oh, I've got a joke. What do librarians call breathalyzers?" Alex paused. "The DUI decimal system! Bad-dum-tss!"

"It seems like you did some drinking yourself," Jasmine said dully. Alex shrugged.

"Maybe a little." Alex flagged down a server and ordered hot tea.

"Since when do you drink tea?" Jasmine looked at her askance. Alex shrugged again and turned her attention on Shoshannah.

"So, Shoshannah, what do you for a living?" Alex asked.

"I'm a CPA, for the Florence Rose Foundation," she said.

"She's an accountant for a non-profit," Jasmine translated unnecessarily. Alex resisted the urge to say something snide to Jasmine and instead remained focused on Shoshannah.

"Cool stuff. Do you like it there?" Alex asked.

"Yeah, it's a nice place to work. What about you?"

"Alex does tech support for one of the CU libraries," Jasmine answered for her. "She does nothing but complain about it, though."

"So, Shoshannah," Alex redirected again. "Jasmine tells me you're the creative type. What kind of art do you do?"

"Oh, Jasmine is so sweet. I'm not that creative," Shoshannah blushed.

"Yes, you are," Jasmine patted Shoshannah's hand affectionately.

"So, what do you do?" Alex asked again.

"Cross-stitch," Shoshannah answered. Alex was confused for a minute. *Cross-stitch? I used to do cross-stitch.* That can't have been what Jasmine was talking about. Jasmine had practically bullied Alex into giving up cross-stitch back when they were first dating. It wasn't *art*, not according to Jasmine.

"Do you, like, design cross-stitch patterns?" Alex asked tentatively. "Or like, do it free-hand?"

"Oh no, I buy the patterns. Like I said, it's not that creative, but I like it. It's meditative," said Shoshannah. Something inside of Alex snapped. She stared, slack-jawed at her girlfriend.

"Are you kidding me, Jasmine?" she huffed. "You went on and on about how she was *'creative,'* and how she *'gets'* you and your art! I thought she was an artist! But she's a fucking *accountant* who does *cross-stitch*?" Alex looked at Shoshannah. "Sorry, this isn't about you. You seem really nice. It's just that..." Alex turned back to Jasmine. Jasmine didn't even look bothered by Alex's rising indignation. That only made Alex angrier. "*Somebody* told me that cross-stitch was 'overblown paint-by-numbers' and could 'hardly be called art.'" Alex felt bitter tears welling up; the back of her throat burned with the effort of keeping them at bay. "And now suddenly it's 'highly creative'? Are you fucking kidding me? Jasmine, if you wanted to break up with me, then you should have had the balls to break up with me. This, what you're doing right now, is *cruel*."

"Alex, I don't want to break up with you," Jasmine said with aggravating calmness. "This isn't about you-"

"It's never about me! Ever! Maybe I want it to be about me now and then, Jasmine. Did you ever think of that?" Alex demanded.

"Alex, you're making a scene," Jasmine said sharply. "Calm down. Why do you always blow everything out of proportion?"

"Out of proportion?"

"Yes! Just like everything else. *Oh poor, Alex. Life is so unfair.* Give me a break," Jasmine rolled her eyes and sighed. "You're just being dramatic. Look, I wanted you to meet Shoshannah because it's important to me that you two got along. I want both of you in my life because I care about both of you." Jasmine gave her a stern don't-be-stupid look, and Alex couldn't think of anything to say. It all felt surreal.

"I'm sorry if I offended you in any way, Alex," Shoshannah said softly. "I really hope we can be friends. Even if it is hard to share our Jasmine."

Shoshannah looked over at Jasmine with this stupid star-struck adoration, this pathetic I'm-just-lucky-to-be-with-her reverence. Alex didn't like it. It made her guts twist uncomfortably. *I don't look that way, do I?* It didn't matter. Alex didn't want to see that look of sickening infatuation on Shoshannah's face.

Not for *her* Jasmine. Jasmine was Alex's girlfriend, even if she was acting like a jerk, she was Alex's jerk, and Alex was done 'sharing.'

"No, I can't," Alex sat back, shaking her head. "I can't share anymore."

"Alex, I told you, I feel this need to connect with multiple partners, I need-"

"Would you listen to what I need for once? I need one partner. One partner who is really there for me. I can't do this," Alex said, feeling her heart break as she did. Jasmine barely reacted. Instead of responding to Alex, she turned to Shoshannah.

"I'm sorry, sweetie, would you give Alex and I a little time. It doesn't look like tonight is going to work out, I'll text you tomorrow, okay?"

"Sure, okay. What about the bill?"

"I've got it. Don't worry. Sorry about all this," Jasmine stood to give her *other* girlfriend a quick kiss farewell. Alex watched the whole exchange in an odd state of numb disbelief. *Didn't I just tell her I was breaking up with her if she didn't dump this girl? Didn't she hear me? How is she so calm?* Alex and Jasmine both silently watched as Shoshannah walked through the restaurant and out the door.

"Why are you doing this to me?" Jasmine hissed, her calm demeanor dropped the instant Shoshannah was gone. "We talked about this. You knew I was seeing other people. You acted like you were supportive. Then you come in here and try and what? Are you just trying to sabotage my relationship with Shoshannah?"

"Your relationship with *Shoshannah*?" Alex screeched incredulously. "Are you kidding? What about your relationship with *me*? Do you even care about it at all?"

"Don't be stupid, of course, I do! If I didn't care, why would I go through all the trouble, risk all the social stigma of being *poly* to stay with you?"

"Wait, what?" Alex was floored by Jasmine's logic. She made it sound as if Alex had somehow forced her into this situation. She stared dumbly at her girlfriend.

"I'm trying to keep us together, Alex," Jasmine explained, head held high in righteous indignation. "I'm taking the steps I need to be fulfilled and be with you at the same time. Because I love you. But you can't be everything to me."

"I don't feel like I'm anything to you right now."

"Don't be stupid-"

"I'm not stupid!" Alex snapped. "Or maybe I am for not saying something sooner. This isn't working for me, and I'm sick of pretending it is. I love you, but I can't keep being the least important person in your life."

"You aren't the least important person in my life, Alex," Jasmine said tartly. "If you feel like you aren't getting what you need from me, you should really try seeing other people too."

"I can't. I tried, and I can't." Alex shook her head. "I'm just not wired that way."

"You tried?" Jasmine raised an eyebrow. "When? With whom?"

"It doesn't matter." Alex didn't want to tell Jasmine about Cait. "The point is that I tried, and I can't be part of a relationship like this."

"Are you really going to break up with me, Alex?" Jasmine stared hard at her like she was daring her to do it. Like she didn't believe Alex would possibly have the guts.

"No. I'm saying that if you want to see other people outside of our relationship, then you'd better break up with me because I'm not okay with it," Alex said stubbornly.

"An ultimatum?" Jasmine sneered. "For crying out loud, Alex. You're acting like a petulant child, you know that?"

"And you're acting like a spoiled brat," Alex snapped. Jasmine's eyes went wide. *Spoiled brat.* Jasmine hated being called 'spoiled' more than anything in the world, and Alex knew that. Jasmine *was* spoiled. She'd grown up with every advantage in the world. Jasmine wouldn't be where she was now without all the support and opportunities her parents gave her. And she resented the hell out of it.

Jasmine felt attacked, persecuted even, for having grown up wealthy. It was her greatest shame. Alex had comforted Jasmine a dozen times as she cried over people *implying* what Alex had just said to her face. *Shit.* Jasmine's eyes filled with tears. Alex wished she could take it back. But it was too late.

"Fuck off, Alex," Jasmine said in a choked whisper. "We're done."

"Jasmine-"

"I said, fuck off!" Jasmine stood up and stomped out. Alex dropped her head into her arms. She could feel the eyes of the other restaurant patrons on her. She didn't want to cry. Not there in public. But she couldn't help the tears that escaped from the corners of her eyes.

Did we really just break up? Is it really over? Alex's heart felt like it was being squeezed until all the blood stopped flowing to the rest of her body. She felt light-headed and realized she was hyperventilating. She forced herself to take slow deep breaths.

"Uh, ma'am, are you alright?"

Alex lifted her head. The server was standing beside the table, looking down at her with a sort of awkwardly sympathetic smile. Alex collected herself. She rubbed her eyes.

"Yeah, sorry for making a scene. Women. What are you gonna do, right?" Alex tried to laugh but it came out strangled. "I guess I'll take the check."

Alex looked down into her tea. It was probably cold by now. *I knew this was coming, so why does it hurt so bad? Why can't I be relieved that it's finally over?* Alex took a deep, shuddering breath. *Over. It's over.* She barely made it out of the restaurant before she began to really cry. The night air was piercingly cold. Alex's head swam with wine and tears. She was too much of a mess to even bike back to her car, much less drive home.

'Are you free tonight? I could use a friend and a ride,' Alex texted Jenny.

'Sorry, I'm running a study session. What's up?'

'Broke up with Jasmine.' Just typing it made fresh tears spill from her eyes.

'Oh shit. I'm sorry. Wine and wallowing tomorrow night?'

'Ok. See u then.' Alex closed her eyes. She couldn't think of anybody else to call. Jasmine and Jenny were basically her whole life outside of work. Now half of that life had just walked away. Sniffling and shivering on the street corner, Alex called a Lyft and went home alone.

Chapter 15

When Alex awoke the next morning, her head was pounding, and her eyes were sore from crying. Her whole body felt dehydrated as if she'd cried out every last ounce of water in her system. To add insult to injury, Alex had to wake up extra early to get a Lyft back to work. At some point, she would need to retrieve her bike from outside the restaurant. *I should just make Jasmine get it; it's really her bike anyway. And she owes me for paying for her fucking date.* Alex grumbled to herself the entire way to work.

When Alex arrived at the library, she stomped straight back to her office and shut herself inside. She turned off notifications on her phone. Alex wasn't ready to deal with people. Not yet. She opened up articles about data migration and lost herself in her research.

When somebody knocked on her door, Alex practically fell out of her chair. She looked at the clock. She'd been down the internet rabbit hole of tech blogs for over three hours. *Oops*. She stood and opened her door. Cait stood outside, arms crossed, an impatient look on her perfect face. She looked Alex up and down. Alex knew she looked like shit, but she couldn't help it. She felt like shit.

"What do you want, Cait?" Alex asked gruffly.

"I want you to give me a little warning if you're going to stand me up," Cait said.

"What?"

"We had a meeting an hour ago, Alex. We talked about it just yesterday. Don't you recall?" Cait narrowed her eyes at Alex. "Are you alright, Alex? You look dreadful."

"I'm fine."

"Where were you then?"

"I was researching for your stupid workaround," Alex snapped. *Why can't she just leave me alone? I missed the meeting, I'm clearly miserable. Does it matter why?*

"*My* stupid workaround?" Cait leaned back and looked at Alex appraisingly. "Alex, what's going on. This workaround was your idea, and it was brilliant. Are you telling me it won't work? Is that what's got you so worked up?"

"I didn't say it wouldn't work. It will, it's just..." Alex's chest was tight with frustration. "It's hard, okay? I need some space to concentrate. This would all be a lot easier if you librarians would just get over yourselves and do things the way everybody else does, you know."

"Get over ourselves?" Cait repeated. "What the fuck is wrong with you today, Alex?"

"None of your damn business," Alex turned away from Cait. "I'm just having a bad day, alright? I'll reschedule the meeting, just leave me alone." She knew she was lashing out at Cait because of her pain over losing Jasmine. But she couldn't help it. She couldn't look into those green eyes with thoughts of Jasmine so fresh and sharp. If she tried to tell Cait what had happened, Alex knew she'd fall to pieces, and she was not going to let herself do that.

"Oh, this is about that *girlfriend* of yours, isn't it?" Cait shocked her by saying.

"How in the hell did you...?" Alex turned to stare at Cait. Cait put a hand on her hip and stared back.

"You left happy hour yesterday to meet her and her ridiculous 'partner' and now today you look like something the cat dragged in. It doesn't take a genius to put two and two together, Alex."

"I don't want to talk about it," Alex turned away again. The tightness in her chest was making regular breathing difficult.

"What happened? Did she finally legitimately dump you?" Cait asked with a derisive snort that brought tears to Alex's eyes. She rounded on Cait.

"Shut up, Cait. Shut up and leave me alone," Alex growled, tears rolling down her cheeks.

"Leave you alone so that you can sit in here and feel sorry for yourself?" Cait shook her head. "Like you did when you first got here? Poor, Alex. Stuck in the library. Poor, Alex. Dumped by her bitch of a girlfriend. Poor Alex, who can never see the opportunities she's pissing away-"

"Get the hell out of my office, Cait!" Alex snapped.

"No, Alex. Why don't you get the hell out of my library!" Cait snapped back.

"What?"

"You heard me. Go back to your precious CUIT if you're going to act like a C-U-*N*-T."

"I'm not-"

"Get over *yourself*, Alex. Forget the 'stupid' work-around and go back where you came from." Cait's voice was low and cold. Alex couldn't believe what she was hearing.

"I can't just go back-"

"Why not? It's what you want, isn't it?" Cait lifted her nose and looked disdainfully at Alex. "You can tell your boss the *evil* librarians kicked you out. You're not getting anything accomplished here anyway."

"I can't believe I thought you were my friend," Alex croaked.

"There are a lot of things I can't believe, Alex," Cait turned on her heel and stormed out of the room, slamming the door shut behind her.

What the fuck just happened? Suddenly Alex had to get out of there. Out of the library, as far away from Cait as she could go. She hastily stuffed her laptop into her bag and made a b-line for the door. Outside fat snowflakes swirled on the light breeze. Alex stuffed her hands in her pockets and began to walk. She walked briskly, in no particular direction.

What is Cait's problem? Why does she seem sweet one day and heartless the next? What the hell is wrong with librarians? Don't they have souls? Feelings? Alex thought that she had a friend in the library from hell. *Apparently not.* Somehow, in some way, that hurt even worse than Jasmine breaking up with her. She'd seen the break-up coming. She hadn't expected this from Cait.

Hot tears ran down Alex's cold cheeks. She felt like she'd lost everything. First, she was banished from the workplace she loved, then she lost her girlfriend, now it looked like she'd lost her only friend in the library. *What's next? Lose my job altogether?*

Alex stopped in her tracks, realizing that she'd been walking toward the student union. The thought of running into Geoff and having to explain for the millionth time why she still wasn't done migrating the library staff was too much. She knew if she did, she would either burst into tears or snap at him, the way she had at Cait. Or worse, tell him *exactly* how she felt about him and his 'directives.' *I would lose my job for sure.*

Alex stood shaking in the cold. She thought about going back to the library. Cait couldn't have been serious. *Could she?* Picturing Cait's cold expression made Alex's heart wrench painfully in her chest.

Maybe I should just go home. It seemed like the least painful option. Alex turned and walked back across the gray campus, past the throngs of students, toward her car. *I can just call in sick.* She had the available leave time. Cait was the only one who had seen her today. She was the only one who would know she wasn't really sick. *Cait wouldn't say anything to anyone about it, would she?* Yesterday Alex would have trusted that she wouldn't. But now Alex wasn't so sure. *What does it matter? I'm probably going to lose my job anyway*.

Alex took the long route to her car to avoid walking directly past the library's big front doors. It was only when Alex arrived at her car that she realized she'd left the key on her desk. *Eejit*, she scolded herself and began to sob. *Damn you, Cait. I really could have used a friend today*. Alex leaned on her car and buried her face in her freezing hands. She cried until a piercing cold breeze brushed the back of her neck, sending her body into a fit of uncontrollable shivering. *I'm going to freeze to death if I just stand here like this.*

Alex didn't want to go back inside and risk facing Cait - pathetic and sniffling as she was. But she didn't have a choice. The wind had picked up. The snow falling from the gray skies had morphed from large lazy flakes to cold white powder that was accumulating rapidly around Alex's feet. She couldn't stay outside crying all day, she'd get hypothermia. Her fingers and toes were already numb with cold.

She crept in the library's side door and took a round-about path back to her office, in an attempt to avoid all human interaction. She didn't bother turning on the lights in the stacks. She knew her way around now, and the less attention she drew to herself, the better. She'd taken a sharp turn to evade Manny when Alex nearly ran headlong into the one person she least wanted to see. Cait.

"Alex..."

"Sorry, I was just leaving," Alex clenched her jaw and tried to push past her.

"Alex, wait. I've been looking for you."

"Why? I thought you wanted me to leave," Alex tried to walk off again, but Cait grabbed her by the arm.

"No, I don't. Alex I… I want to apologize." Cait said, her voice coming out oddly. Alex looked at her. Cait's face was hard to read in the dark stacks. "I'm sorry, I should not have snapped at you as I did this morning. That was uncalled for." Cait was looking directly into Alex's eyes, and Alex found she couldn't look away. *It wasn't totally uncalled for though, was it?*

"I shouldn't have told you to get over yourself," Alex said contritely.

"No, but I over-reacted, and I'm sorry. I hope that… Oh, Alex, you're shivering." Cait's hand on Alex's arm moved to squeeze her shoulder. "You're shaking like a leaf. How long were you outside?" Cait asked. Before Alex could answer, Cait put a hand to Alex's cheek. "Jaysus, you're freezing cold. Did you not have a hat? Or gloves?" Cait took Alex's hands and held them between her own.

"I'm okay, really," Alex protested, but she didn't pull her hands from Cait's. Cait was so warm. Cait brought their hands up to her mouth to blow hot breath on them. Her lips lightly brushed the tips of Alex's fingers, and Alex's body began to tingle with prickles of heat thawing her body from the inside. There was a moment, a fleeting few seconds where Cait stood still, holding her hands and looking into her eyes when Alex felt her heart stop inside her chest.

"We should get you some tea," Cait said, dropping Alex's hands. The second Cait dropped her hands, Alex's heartbeat resumed its normal rhythm, and she began to shiver again.

"I can't go into the staff room, I'm too much of a mess," Alex protested, although hot tea did sound good.

"I'll fetch it for you," Cait smiled. "Meet you back in your office then? You know the way now?"

"Yeah, I think I finally got it figured out, thanks," Alex said with a soft snort.

"Alright, I'll see you shortly," Cait turned and disappeared into the dim stacks. Alex made her way back to her office. Emotionally she was all turned around, she couldn't make heads or tails of what was going on with Cait. It was all overwhelming.

Alex stood just inside the door of her office and stared at her desk. She didn't want to sit there. She didn't have the emotional energy to even pretend like she would be able to get any more work done today. *I'm going to get fired for sure. Jasmine was right. I'm not career-driven at all.*

Instead of sitting in her chair, Alex leaned her back against the wall and slid down to the floor. *Why can't my life just go the way I want for once?* She tilted her head back and closed her eyes. *Poor Alex. Always feeling sorry for herself,* she scolded herself, just as Jasmine had, just as Cait had. *I am so pathetic. Here I am, sitting on the floor like a child, feeling sorry for myself.*

"Are you asleep there?"

Alex opened her eyes; Cait stood in the doorway, two steaming mugs in her hands. Alex took the one offered her.

"May I sit with you?" Cait asked.

"Yeah, if you want." Alex was surprised when Cait actually sat down beside her on the floor. Cait wasn't the type to be crawling around under desks like Alex, her clothes always looked pressed and perfect. Nonetheless, Cait settled herself on the thin office carpet and leaned against the wall. They both drank their tea in silence for a while.

"You know, I never liked tea before I started working here," Alex said. "Jasmine was always trying to get me to drink tea with her, but I never liked the tea she bought, and she only bought the one type."

"Let me guess she drinks *jasmine* tea?"

"How'd you know?"

"I haven't met her, but I know the type," Cait said. She gazed out in the distance for a moment, like her mind had gone somewhere else. Then she sighed and rolled her head to look at Alex. "Your ex-girlfriend really loves herself, doesn't she?"

"Yeah," Alex snorted. "She does."

"You should be happy to be done with her."

"I spent almost two years of my life with her," Alex said, feeling distinctly *unhappy* thinking about all that time she'd invested in her relationship with Jasmine, all for nothing. "Why would I be happy that it's over?"

"*Jaysus*, two years? With that horrid excuse for a girlfriend?" Cait shook her head. "Well, maybe you're not exactly happy, not yet, but at least you should be relieved. Two years is a long time, but you're finally free."

"You say free, I say alone."

"You don't have to be alone, Alex," Cait said softly. "Not if you don't want to be."

Alex looked at Cait. *Is she saying what I think she's saying?* Alex's heart skipped a beat. She could see the question clearly in Cait's eyes. *Would you like to be with me?* She did, or at least part of her did. But not now, not while the wounds of her breakup with Jasmine were still so raw. It was too much.

"Cait, I-"

"Alex, wait," Cait stopped her. "I don't mean to put you on the spot. You deserve time to recover. I just want you to know that I'm here, as a friend, or a colleague, or whatever it is you need right now."

"Thanks," Alex smiled. "I appreciate that."

Alex was amazed by how much better she felt after sitting and sipping tea on the floor with Cait. She hardly got any work done, but by the end of the day, she left the office feeling oddly accomplished. She'd made it through her first day of life after Jasmine.

'We still on for wine and wallowing?' Jenny texted. Alex had almost forgotten.

'Yeah, I'll be right over.'

Alex and Jenny spent the evening re-watching *The IT Crowd*, drinking wine, and making Markus fetch them snacks from the kitchen. Markus was a great boyfriend. Jenny was lucky - a fact Alex reminded her of more and more frequently the drunker she got.

"If you weren't a man, I'd totally do you," Alex told Markus as he brought them pizza bagels and another bottle of wine. Alex waved her hand in the general direction of Markus's crotch. "It's too bad about that whole penis thing you've got going on."

"Hey, I like that 'whole penis thing,'" Jenny shoved Alex. "Doubly-so if it keeps you from trying to steal my man."

"Yeah, it's a hard-pass on the man thing," Alex squeezed her eyes shut and stuck out her tongue. "But I wouldn't mind a girlfriend who brought me pizza bagels. You got a sister, Markus?"

"You know he doesn't," Jenny rolled her eyes. "I bet there are tons of women out there just dying to bring Alex Rossi junk food. You just haven't met them yet. Not everybody is a stuck-up hipster princess like Jasmine, you know. You should get out there and try to meet somebody new." Jenny reached out and refilled Alex's glass. "Find somebody who will pour your wine *and* sleep with you."

"Maybe I already did," Alex said quietly, thinking about Cait pouring her wine at the happy hour and bringing her tea in the office. She thought about what Cait had said today. *Am I really ready for somebody new?*

"What?" Jenny asked, blinking at her, eyebrows raised in question. Alex shook her head.

"Nothing," she said. "Hey, Netflix is binge-shaming us again. We're still watching, right?"

"Hell yeah," Jenny pointed the remote at the TV. "Come on, Netflix, why you gotta be so judgy?"

"I don't know how you can watch that show," Markus said as the next episode of the British sitcom began to play. "I can hardly understand a word they're saying."

"Markus can't hear the words through the trees," Jenny giggled. "Or the forest through the accent."

"You're mixing your metaphor with real words again," Alex snorted.

"You know what I mean," Jenny waved a hand at her. "He does better learning whole new languages than listening to people speak English with funny accents."

"Oh, you should hear Cait's accent when she starts drinking," Alex giggled. "It's so cute in this fiery Irish-girl-in-a-pub-about-to-start-a-brawl sort of way. *Jaysus, Alex. Yer so fulla shite, ye'd tink yer arse was goin' in reverse.*" Alex threw herself into the imitation. Jenny and Markus both cracked up. Alex could feel her face warm as she grinned.

"You really should meet her, she's a riot," Alex said when Markus and Jenny had stopped laughing.

"Hot and funny, huh?" Jenny eyed Alex. "So, are you gonna actually put the moves on her, now that Jasmine is out of the picture?"

"Maybe. I think Jasmine needs to get a little further out of frame, though. I don't want it to end up like last time and find myself thinking about Jasmine while Cait-" Alex stopped. She hadn't told Jenny about her *connection* with Cait in the bathroom. She'd been too embarrassed.

"While Cait what? What last time?" Jenny picked up on Alex's omission right away, and Alex had no choice but to spill the whole story.

"Okay, now I'm really confused why you're not jumping to get with her," Jenny poked at Alex. "It sounds like she wants you as badly as you want her."

"I just need time." Alex shook her head. "Like I said, I need to get Jasmine fully evicted from my brain-space before I can invite Cait in."

"How long is that going to take?" Jenny asked.

"I don't know. One day at a time, I guess."

"Well, here's to one day down," Jenny clinked her glass against Alex's.

"One good day at that," Alex agreed.

Chapter 16

That good day was followed by another and another. When Jasmine texted Alex a week later to schedule a time to exchange the things they'd left at each other's places, Alex immediately worried that seeing Jasmine might derail her progress getting over the relationship.

'What if we somehow end up getting back together??' Alex texted Jenny as she waited for Jasmine to show up at her apartment. She was sitting on her sofa, nervously tapping her foot and staring at the box of toiletries, books, and clothing she had packed to give back to her ex.

'Do you want to get back together?' texted Jenny.

'No!'

'Then don't! It's not like she's gonna bewitch you or something. Chill.'

That didn't reassure Alex in the least. Somehow Jasmine had bewitched her into staying in a troubling relationship for far too long in the past. Alex didn't trust herself not to fall for Jasmine's beauty and manipulation again.

When Jasmine arrived, the first thing that struck Alex was the complete lack of attraction she felt for her former girlfriend. Jasmine was still objectively beautiful, Alex supposed. Nothing had changed that she could have explicitly called out. But the allure was gone.

"Hello, *Lexie*," Jasmine said tartly. "I'm glad we can do this civilly. I want to thank you for not texting me, begging to get back together. I appreciate the restraint you've shown."

"Huh?" Alex hadn't 'shown restraint.' She just didn't want to get back together.

"It's been really good for me to have space," Jasmine continued before Alex could get a word in, smiling as if she didn't notice Alex's utter bewilderment. "How have you been?" she asked.

"I'm good." Alex shrugged. Jasmine looked at her like she expected something. Alex stared back, silently. When it became clear that Alex wasn't going to say anything further, Jasmine let out a small huff

"Great. Fine. So, are those my things?" Jasmine asked, indicating the box on the coffee table. Alex picked it up.

"Yup, let me know if you think you're missing anything," Alex said as she handed Jasmine the box. Jasmine set it down and shuffled through its contents. She pulled out two strongly scented candles - Jasmine's favorites - jasmine and patchouli.

"These were a *gift*, Alex. You don't need to return them," Jasmine held them out to Alex. Alex had only ever lit those candles when Jasmine was around. She had no intention of using them again. Ever.

"I thought they were just your way of telling me you thought my apartment smelled bad," Alex said coolly, shoving her hands in her pockets to make clear that she wouldn't be taking them back.

"Well, it still smells bad," Jasmine snapped in retort. Alex shook her head. She knew her apartment smelled fine; Jasmine just had to get in that last dig.

Those types of comments used to hurt, but not anymore.

"You know," said Alex. "You're kind of a jerk sometimes, Jasmine. But I don't care what you think. You're not my girlfriend, and I don't want my apartment to smell like you are."

"You're so childish, Alex." Jasmine threw the candles back in the box. "Whatever. Fine. Here's your shit." Jasmine slid a shopping bag across the floor with her foot. "Goodbye, Alex. And good luck."

"Goodbye, Jasmine."

When Alex closed the door on Jasmine, it was like closing a chapter in her life. Alex felt as if a weight had been lifted. A weight she didn't even know she'd been carrying. *Cait and Jenny were right. Being free of Jasmine is a relief.*

At that moment, Alex made up her mind to give a relationship with Cait a real try. She felt ready. She'd taken her time to mourn her relationship with Jasmine - to put it in the past. She wasn't sad anymore. That book was closed and shelved, and she was ready to move on. Cait was everything Alex could imagine wanting out of a girlfriend. Beautiful, smart, and above all, *kind*. Even if she was a librarian. Alex went to bed that night filled with optimism and thoughts of copper hair and porcelain skin.

Lust in the Stacks

Chapter 17

"I think I'm going to really go for it with Cait," Alex said, the second she and Charles were seated. They were at Taste of India, their favorite eat-yourself-into-a-coma lunch buffet near campus. Alex had dragged Charles out to lunch, specifically to announce her intentions to her long-distance work husband.

"The librarian?" Charles asked, blonde eyebrows raised. Alex nodded. Charles picked up a forkful of rice and butter chicken and shoved it in his mouth. "Like, really date her?" he asked as he chewed. "Or just bang her?"

"I dunno, whatever happens," Alex shrugged, feigning nonchalance. She ripped off a large bite of naan and chewed slowly to give herself time to think. *Oh shit, what if she really only wanted to hook up, and I've over-thinking this whole thing?* Alex hadn't considered that. Ever since she'd broken up with Jasmine, her mind had been on the whole 'girlfriend' concept. But now that she thought about it, their previous tryst in the bathroom didn't exactly scream 'deep relationship material.' But that was before they'd gotten to know one another...

"I wouldn't date her," Charles counseled. "Nookie in the closet is one thing-"

"I don't do anything 'in the closet,' dude." Alex said with a wink and a wry smile. Charles snorted.

"Yeah, yeah, yeah. You're the queen of the lesbians. Whatever." Charles waved his fork at her. "What I'm saying is that if Geoff finds out you're sleeping with the enemy, you're toast. You're already his least favorite person, like ever. He blames you for all the libraries resisting the migration."

"That's not my fault!" Alex protested, almost spitting out her mouthful of food.

"You're the one who talked to the director," Charles pointed out.

"Geoff should have talked to her in the first place! They have a point, you know. If he'd taken their input before making a decision-"

"I don't recommend saying that to Geoff." Charles squinted at her. "Whose side are you on anyway? You turning *librarian* on us?"

"I'm not on anybody's 'side.' I'm trying to help," Alex grumbled. "It had already all gone to shit by the time I talked to Mandy anyway. Besides, that has nothing to do with me and Cait. Sleeping with her isn't going to change anything about the damn migration project."

"Whatever. I'm just saying, if you can't keep it in your pants, at least keep it in the library." Charles went back to his food. "There's no way Geoff would believe you were doing your job objectively if he knew you were *dating* a librarian."

As they ate in silence, Alex considered Charles's warning. She really liked Cait. But did she like her enough to put her job in even more jeopardy? *What if Cait doesn't even want a relationship? What if this is just a work-place hook-up to her?* If it was just a workplace hookup, it might still be worth it. If they could keep it confined to the library, there'd be no reason Geoff would have to find out. If it became more, maybe it would be worth losing her job.

Hell, my job might be toast anyway, it's not as if I've made any functional progress on the migration. Alex's technical solution was still as theoretical as her romance with Cait. *I can put them both to the test today.* Alex burped a curry and garlic burp; she looked down at her empty plate and rubbed her full belly. *Okay, I can put them to the test tomorrow.*

Chapter 18

The next morning, the second she was done answering urgent emails and support calls, Alex went looking for Cait. The library felt deserted as Alex wandered the stacks. All the lights were out. After searching nearly every floor, Alex found Cait in the back of the archives, bent over one of the four heavy wooden tables, peering at some old book. She looked somehow even more ravishing than ever. Her copper hair shone red-gold in the warm light from the desk lamp beside her. The way she was bent Alex could just see down the top of her v-neck sweater. But Alex wasn't staring at her chest, as worthy of staring as it was. Alex was looking at her lips. Her perfect, plush pink lips. Every cell in Alex's body was screaming at her to kiss those lips.

"Hey, Cait," Alex said. Cait started, and her head shot up.

"*Jaysus*, Alex. Don't sneak up on me like that. You nearly scared me to death," Cait said, hand on over her heart. Cait took a deep breath; Alex watched Cait's long delicate fingers pressing against her heaving breasts.

"Sorry, I wasn't trying to sneak up on you." Alex tore her eyes from Cait's chest and approached the desk. "But that was kind of funny, you jumped like three feet."

"Ah feck off," Cait swatted at her.

"What are you looking at that has you so enraptured?" Alex asked, moving to stand close next to Cait, close enough that their shoulders brushed lightly together. She could smell the sweet scent of Cait's hair, feel the warmth of her body.

"Oh, this?" Cait gestured down at the book, which lay open on the table before them. "It's an illustrated bible from the eighteenth century. But I wouldn't say I was *enraptured*," Cait turned and smiled coyly at Alex. "It's hardly the most alluring sight in the room."

"Oh?" Alex's breathing grew shallow as they stood, so close together, Cait's eyes locked on hers.

"What do you find alluring here in this old dusty room?" Alex asked in a voice barely above a whisper.

"You, Alex."

"I was hoping you were going to say that," Alex barely got the words out before she leaned in and kissed Cait. Cait's lips were even softer than Alex remembered. Their touch ignited a firestorm of heat and passion that radiated from her chest to her toes. Alex slid a hand around Cait's waist, pulled her close, and kissed her deeper, her tongue slipping between Cait's lips. Cait's lips parted, and their tongues met; she tasted of mint and honey. Alex's whole body responded to the wonderful sensation of Cait's mouth on hers. Her skin tingled with goosebumps, and she could feel her nipples harden. Alex couldn't get enough. She ran her hand up the back of Cait's neck, burying her fingers in her hair. She pulled her in closer, kissed her harder, faster.

Cait's hands slid down to grip Alex's ass, and Alex felt a surge in the quickly spreading wetness between her legs. Alex moaned as Cait pulled their bodies together. The heat of pleasure pulsed in Alex as they moved against one another; it was excruciatingly teasing - standing there. Alex wanted to climb on the table and get Cait between her legs. Her clit seemed to burn, almost white-hot with need. But the hunger to taste Cait burned hotter. Alex lifted Cait onto the table, pushing her skirt up and over her hips. Alex slid a hand between Cait's legs.

"Don't you ever wear underpants?" Alex asked when she found only bare skin.

"Not if I can help it," Cait grinned. Alex groaned, her arousal growing as she touched Cait. She lightly ran her fingers just inside the edges of Cait's labia. *Oh god, she's so wet.* Alex pressed her thumb against Cait's clit; Cait gasped. Alex's fingers slid easily inside of Cait's wetness. Being inside of her was such a fantastic feeling; it made Alex's whole body throb. Cait moaned and bucked her hips against Alex's hand while pulling her head in for a series of deep kisses. Alex rubbed her thumb against Cait's clit and curled her fingers. Cait's head fell back, and Alex could see that she was biting her lip to keep from screaming. Alex withdrew her fingers and licked them; the taste of Cait was intoxicating. Alex's mouth began to salivate. She wanted more, more of Cait. Alex pulled the librarian to the edge of the table and kneeled before her.

"May I?" she asked, looking up. Cait nodded enthusiastically, and Alex lowered her mouth onto Cait.

Alex was like an animal, mad with thirst, who had just found the oasis. She pressed her tongue against Cait like she would never get enough of her. It had been so long since Alex had been with somebody new, she reveled in the process of finding all the right spots - all the ways she could make Cait buck and gasp. Cait moaned low and deep in her throat. *Can moans have accents?* Alex wondered. Because somehow even Cait's moaning sounded somehow *Irish.*

"Oh, god, yes," Cait groaned, her voice growing louder with each flick of Alex's tongue.

"Shhhh," Alex whispered, pulling back slightly to peer up at Cait. "You have to be quiet in the library."

"Jaysus, Alex, don't stop," Cait begged. The sound of Alex's name on Caits lips sent another jolt of pleasure through Alex. Her underpants had to be absolutely *soaked* by now. Alex smiled and waited for a second longer, just to hear Cait whine before lowering her head back into place. Cait's whole body shook with silent screams when she came.

"Don't forget to breathe, Cait," Alex said as she got to her feet. Cait took a couple gasping breaths before she grabbed Alex, pulled her onto the table, and kissed her.

"That," she breathed between kisses, "was amazing." Cait unbuttoned Alex's pants and slipped her hand inside. Alex moaned against Cait's lips as Cait's fingers slid down between her legs. Alex was so turned on, it had been so long since somebody had touched her, Alex began to come almost immediately.

"Oh fuck," Alex whispered. She buried her face in Cait's shoulder to muffle her cries. Cait continued to finger her even as Alex's body shook with orgasms that rumbled over her like a growing avalanche. "Oh, fuck. Oh god, Cait, you have to- Oh!" Alex gasped as the avalanche overtook her. Alex put her hand over Cait's, holding it still against her as the deluge of pleasure rendered her incapable of speech.

"Now, don't you forget to breathe," Cait slowly withdrew her hand.

"*Jaysus*." Alex groaned when she caught her breath. "Why did it take me so long to do this?"

"I dunno, Alex, I thought that was pretty quick myself," Cait teased.

"Seriously, I should've never turned you away the first time," Alex said, sitting up and looking at Cait. Laying on the table, her hair splayed around her head, cheeks flushed, Cait was stunning, almost super-humanly beautiful.

"I'm glad you *came* around, so to speak," Cait laughed. "That was amazing. Your tongue is deadly, Alex."

"If you think that was good, I can't wait to get you someplace a bit more private," Alex grinned down at her. She ran her hand along the bare skin between Cait's skirt and sweater. She was so soft and warm. Cait closed her eyes.

"Mmmm, I'm knackered," Cait yawned.

"You can't fall asleep now."

"Why not?"

"Well, for one, you're lying on a table in the middle of the archives," Alex pointed out. Cait flicked her wrist dismissively as if this was of absolutely no consequence. Alex laughed and ran her thumb across Cait's navel. "Also, I thought we could test my migration solution today."

"Really?" Cait asked, opening one eye.

"Yeah, I thought maybe we could migrate your computer." Alex's fingers traced Cait's abs. It was difficult to think about computers when she would rather spend all day exploring Cait's body. *Why not both?* Alex gave Cait a coy smile. "Come on, let's go up to your office… I'm sure we could do something to get rid of Joan while we… migrate."

Alex let her hand 'migrate' further up under Cait's sweater until her fingers reached the edge of her bra. Cait let out a sound that was half sigh, half whimper.

"Alright, Alex, let's go tell Joan to feck off and do some 'migrating.'"

Chapter 19

Over the next week, things between Alex and Cait went from hot to scorching. Any second they had free during the day, they found each other. It wasn't all sex; they had lunch together, they talked and laughed together. But there was also sex, and the sex was amazing.

Ironically, the only space within the Cowling Library for the Humanities that they could have had totally to themselves - Alex's office - was off-limits. Cait firmly refused; all the monitors Alex had set up freaked her out. Cait said she felt like they were watching her, and no matter how many times Alex promised that she'd covered up the one camera, Cait would not do it in her office. Bathrooms, stairwells, dusty back corners of the stacks - all of these were on the table, so to speak. But not Alex's office.

'Better to be caught than recorded,' Cait had insisted when she dragged Alex from the privacy of her office to revisit the 'jacks' where they had first kissed.

Alex grinned at the memory as she uncovered her webcam to prepare for her virtual entrance into the CUIT check-in meeting. She logged into the video conference. Alex was early for once and had to sit nervously as she watched everybody file into the room and take their seats. Alex was prepared. More prepared than she'd likely ever been for a meeting. She wanted so badly for it to go well. The test on Cait's computer had been a success, the library director was on-board, now all she needed was for Geoff to wrap his simple mind around the concept. Alex was jumpy with nerves when it was her turn to speak. She laid it all out clearly and professionally.

"You're sure this little 'solution' will work?" Geoff questioned Alex after she'd gone over the technical details.

"We did a test… *migration*," Alex had to fight to keep her face straight and her voice steady. The memories of that afternoon 'migrating' in Cait's office made her want to giggle like a schoolgirl. She cleared her throat. "We did one of the staff computers, and it seems to have worked."

"You keep saying 'we,' who's 'we'?" Geoff asked.

"Cait Murphy, the librarian I've been uh," Alex coughed. "...working with." Alex may have imagined it, but she thought she could hear Charles snicker in the background. *Stay professional*, Alex reminded herself. "So, now that we know it works, do you think this is a solution we could implement throughout the whole library system?"

"I'll consider it," said Geoff. "In the meantime, I want you back in central CUIT."

"What?" Alex was stunned. She hadn't been prepared for that. Her mind went immediately to Cait. "But I still have work-"

"Be back at your desk in the student union Monday morning," Geoff interrupted. He wrapped up the rest of the meeting, and Alex signed off. She sat in her silent office, not knowing what to feel. She should be thrilled to go back to her desk. Her real desk at her real job. But she wasn't.

What will happen with Cait? Alex didn't know if what she and Cait had together was moving towards a real relationship, or if it was just a workplace fling that would fall apart once she left the library.

I have to suck it up and have the relationship talk. Fuck. Alex typed out a long text to Cait and then deleted it.

'You free?' she typed instead and hit send.

'My whole afternoon is booked with meetings, sorry.'

'Can I see you after work?' Alex held her breath as she sent the text. That was it. That was the start of the relationship conversation. Can this exist outside of work? Cait took maddeningly long to respond. Alex tapped her foot impatiently against the side of the desk. *If I were back at my cube, Charles would yell at me*. He hated repetitive noises like that. Alex's foot tapped faster. *It'll be nice to see Charles, but I'm going to miss having my own office.* Her phone buzzed. *Cait.*

'I'd love that. Meet for drinks at Union Tap?'

'Be there at 5:01!' Alex texted back. Union Tap was a bar just off campus that staff often went to for post-work happy hours. It was about as relationship-status-neutral as possible. If anything, it leaned in the not-a-relationship direction. *Maybe we are just colleagues who bang on the sly.* If that was the case,

Alex was going to be a lot sadder about moving back into the student union. Alex tried to think of a way to tell Cait about the move that might elicit a response that would give Alex a clue as to Cait's feelings.

You could just be a grown-up about it and ask her, Alex told herself. She shook her head. She knew she'd feel like a total idiot if she asked, and Cait laughed at the idea of being a couple. The more Alex thought about it, the more laughable it seemed, a goddess of a woman like Cait being tied down to a geek like Alex. *I have to figure it out tonight.*

Alex opened the door to Union Tap and glanced around the moderately crowded bar. There was no sign of Cait's copper hair. Alex settled into a two-seat high-top and ordered a beer. She checked her phone. 5:05. *Be patient, she said she had a lot of meetings.*

Alex played solitaire on her phone and slowly sipped her beer as she waited for Cait. When the beer had been sipped down to nothing, Alex rechecked the time. 5:32.

'Hey are you coming to the Tap?' she texted Cait.

'Shit! I'm so sorry! I completely forgot. I'm still in my office. I'll be right there!'

Alex's heart sank. Cait had forgotten all about their first 'date' outside of work. That felt like another tally mark in the not-a-relationship column. Alex wondered if she should just tell Cait not to bother. *No. Even if it isn't a relationship, having drinks together tonight would be fun.* It wasn't as if Alex had any other plans.

'Ok. See ya soon!' Alex ordered a second beer and went back to her game. Before Alex's second drink arrived, Cait showed up at the table. She smelled of cold air, her face flushed pink. She was flustered and out of breath.

"I am so incredibly sorry, Alex," Cait said as she unwrapped her scarf and removed her coat.

"I've stood you up twice, it's karmic justice," Alex shrugged.

"Nonetheless, I'm so sorry." Cait slid into her seat. "I got wrapped up in my research for this English class. Did you know that the first book printed in Irish was actually printed in Scotland?"

"Of course, doesn't everybody know that?" Alex grinned. "Hey, what do a librarian and a sex addict have in common?"

"I said I was sorry for being late, no need for personal attacks," Cait raised an eyebrow at her.

"Their favorite activities are between the covers," Alex drummed the table.

"An interesting choice of words given that we've been just about everywhere *but* between the covers," Cait winked. Alex grinned.

"We could change that, you know."

"Oh, is that what you meant when you asked to see me 'after work'? Do you want to get out of here then?" Cait asked, moving to rise. Rushing off for more sex, rather than staying for drinks and maybe dinner, seemed like another not-a-relationship move.

"Actually, I already ordered another beer," Alex said quickly. "And I thought maybe you'd like to get dinner."

"That would be grand." Cait settled back into her seat. *Okay, maybe this is a date.* Alex didn't feel sure yet; Cait could just be going along with what Alex had suggested. That didn't mean she *wanted* it to be a date. *Say something useful*, Alex told herself, *something that could give a hint about how Cait really feels*. Alex wracked her brain as Cait flagged for a waiter and ordered a drink.

"Geoff wants me back in the student union," Alex finally blurted out. "I have to leave the library."

"Oh," Cait said softly. Her perfect face went stone still - completely unreadable. Alex looked into her eyes. *What are you thinking?*

"He wants me back at my desk Monday," Alex added when she realized Cait wasn't going to say anything. "He didn't say why."

"Did you tell him that the migration worked on my computer?" Cait asked collegially.

"Yeah, I did. He said he'd 'consider' implementing it, then told me to come back to central CUIT."

"How do you feel about that?" Cait asked. That was the question, wasn't it? *I'd feel a lot better if I knew it didn't mean losing you*, Alex thought. She was too nervous to say that outright.

"I dunno," Alex shrugged. "I want to go back to my old job, but I feel like… like I'm leaving things… unfinished. With you. You know, in the library."

"I hope you can come back and finish things," Cait said, no hint of double-entendre in her voice. "Once Mandy and Geoff have signed off on your migration plan, mind."

"Yeah," Alex nodded. This felt distinctly like a work conversation. Not a relationship conversation. *Come on, stop being chicken-shit and actually talk about what you're here to talk about.* "Speaking of migrations…" Alex took a deep breath and reached across the table to take Cait's hand. "I'd like to keep seeing you. Even when I'm not in the library. Would you?"

"I'd like that very much," Cait intertwined their fingers and rubbed her thumb across Alex's palm. Alex's heart fluttered in her chest. *Okay, this feels like a relationship moment.* Alex may not have used the word 'girlfriend' in her question, but she could get to that later.

The positive relationship-y feeling lasted through dinner. With each minute and each drink, it grew increasingly difficult for Alex to keep her hands off of Cait. Cait appeared to be having the same difficulty; she stroked Alex's arm, held her hand, nudged her leg. Each touch was teasing in its innocence.

The moment they stepped out of the bar into the brisk night air, Alex pulled Cait aside and kissed her. Despite the cold of the winter, Alex was glowing with warmth and affection as Cait kissed her back. A group of college boys passed by them on the sidewalk. One of the guys whistled at them.

"Can I join the fun?" he jeered.

"Fuck off," Cait flipped him the bird. The guys laughed. Alex bristled. *Why do men insist on being such turds?* She took Cait by the hand and walked briskly in the opposite direction.

"God, I hate that. 'Join the fun'?" Alex made a gagging face. "Guh."

"Let's don't let some gobshite frat boy ruin our fun." Cait pulled her in and kissed her again. Cait's kisses felt so good; Alex wanted more.

"I think we could have a lot more *fun* back at my place," Alex suggested.

"Between the covers?" Cait asked with a laugh.

"Maybe." Alex grinned. "If we make it that far past the front door."

"Lead the way, Alexandria," Cait squeezed her hand.

"You're lucky you're beautiful," Alex warned. "Nobody calls me 'Alexandria' and gets away with it."

"Who says I'm trying to get away with it?" Cait kissed Alex, biting her bottom lip as she did. "Maybe I want to be punished."

There was a rush a heat between Alex's legs. She closed her eyes, and her head swam with beer and lust. She opened her eyes and looked at Cait, who was looking at her with a small, seductive smile curling her lips. The heat between Alex's legs throbbed, begging for attention.

"I have got to get you home," Alex all but carried Cait back to her apartment. When Alex closed the apartment door behind them, Cait immediately drew her close. She reached back and pulled out Alex's ponytail. Alex sighed and closed her eyes as Cait ran her fingers through her hair.

"You look so beautiful with it down," Cait cooed. Alex opened her eyes. Cait was looking at her with unmistakable lust in her expression; Alex couldn't remember the last time somebody looked at her with that much intense wanting. Cait ran her fingers through Alex's hair. "Why don't you ever wear it down?" she asked.

"I dunno," Alex shrugged. She could feel her cheeks burn, uncomfortable with the compliment, but enjoying it nonetheless. "It's too much of a hassle. Putting it up is easier. I've considered cutting it all off-"

"Don't you dare," Cait tightened her grip on Alex's hair and pulled her in for a kiss. A surge of electric excitement shot through Alex. *Okay, don't cut the hair, got it.* Her knees felt weak. *Bedroom.* Alex put her hands on Cait's hips and steered her through the apartment.

Cait released her grip on Alex's hair and began to take off Alex's clothes. She pulled Alex's shirt up and over her head, slid off her bra, and pushed her down onto the bed. Alex struggled to push her unbound hair away from her eyes and mouth, as Cait undid her pants and pulled them off, along with her underpants. Cait kneeled over her on the bed. Alex pulled at her, but Cait shook her head.

"You're so delicious, Alex, I just want to take a moment to appreciate you," Cait's eyes were wandering across Alex's naked body. Alex realized this was the first time she'd ever actually been naked in front of Cait. She shivered despite the warmth of the room.

"No fair," Alex protested. "The least you can do is to return the favor."

"I suppose fair is fair." Cait moved to stand beside the bed. Slowly she unbuttoned each button of her thin, pink blouse with deliberate, unhurried motions. Alex's eyes followed her slender fingers, entranced. When Cait reached the last button, she slipped it off her shoulders and let it fall to the floor. Cait was wearing a bra today, Alex noted with some disappointment. Cait grinned at her as if she knew exactly what Alex was thinking. When Cait didn't reach to remove her bra, Alex let out a small whine.

"Patience, Alex," Cait said in a low, hushed voice. Slowly she unzipped her skirt, and it too succumbed to gravity, landing in a puddle at Cait's feet. Cait took two steps and kicked the skirt away. She hooked her fingers in the top of her leggings and with slow teasing movements, pulled them down, bending to free one foot, and then the other. She flipped her long hair back as she straightened. Alex let out a small sigh of appreciation.

Alex entirely forgot about her own nakedness as her eyes greedily took in Cait's. Alex's gaze followed the perfect curves of her body, from her smooth calves, up along her thighs, pausing to appreciate the place where her legs met and remember the taste of her. Her mouth watered at the memory. Cait shifted her weight, and Alex's eyes continued upward - over the curve of her hips, up, up… Cait unclasped and removed her bra, exposing her impossibly perfect breasts with their taut pink nipples. Standing there before her, Cait was a goddess - perfect as if she were devised to be carved in marble.

"Holy fuck, do you have any idea how hot you are?" Alex sighed. She looked into Cait's wonderfully familiar and endlessly radiant face.

"The way you look at me, that makes me feel incredibly... *hot*," Cait's lips turned up in a carnal smile that sent another shiver up Alex's spine. Cait slowly crawled onto the bed.

"Are you cold?" she asked.

"No- oh!" Alex gasped as Cait lowered her mouth onto one nipple, biting it lightly. Alex moaned. Cait nudged Alex's legs apart. Alex moaned again as Cait's fingers found her wetness. She dipped her fingers in it, spread it. Then she opened her own legs and straddled Alex, moving their legs until the angle was just right and pressed herself against her.

"Is this good?" Cait asked as she began to roll her hips against her.

"Oh yeah," Alex breathed. She pulled Cait's head down and kissed her feverishly. Cait moved her body faster, and Alex's kisses grew distracted. She arched her back, pushing her hips harder against Cait. A small wave crested within her, and Alex froze, shaking.

Cait continued to roll her hips. Alex grabbed her firm white ass and squeezed in rhythm with Cait's bucking. Cait groaned and whimpered; her hands gripped Alex's thighs as her movements took on a focused intensity. Alex looked up at her. She was panting and sweating, her eyes squeezed closed in concentration on her pleasure. Alex forgot her own body for a moment, entranced by Cait's beauty and primal sensuality. Cait suddenly threw her head back.

"Oh god, Alex," she cried out. Her body shuddered, and she fell into Alex's arms. Alex ran her hands along Cait's back. It was cool and damp with sweat. Alex walked her fingers along Cait's spine, and she shivered.

"Mmmm, that was so fucking sexy," Alex whispered. She kissed the soft skin of Cait's shoulder, savoring the salt of her sweat as her lips worked their way toward Cait's neck. "Have fun?"

"Oh, yes, Alex," Cait lifted her head. "But there's a lot more fun to be had yet."

"Yeah?" Alex asked with a smile. Cait kissed her.

"Mm-hmm," Cait bit Alex's lip again. "We've barely begun."

Cait kissed and licked a long trail down from Alex's lips, along her neck, across her collarbone, down between her breasts, pausing to kiss each nipple before continuing her journey south over Alex's abdomen. Alex watched until Cait's lips disappeared between her legs, at which point Alex dropped her head back and sighed.

"Ohhh," she breathed. There were no words for the way Cait's mouth on her made her feel. It was an all-consuming sensation of warmth and pleasure that spread outward to fill her whole body with light and joy. And at the center of that warmth was Cait's tongue, moving, like a finger tracing words in the sand, spelling out the very definition of *bliss* with soft, deliberate articulation.

When Cait pushed inside of her, adding another layer to the already overwhelming mix of sensation, Alex feared she might explode or melt or some unholy combination of both. How could her body possibly contain this much feeling without coming apart at the seams? Cait made Alex unstable in the best way - tearing her apart at the molecular level until her every atom glowed white-hot - like the next touch could send her into full a nuclear reaction that would level the city and leave the whole earth quaking.

When the crescendo peaked, and Alex came, she let out a loud, definitely-not-in-the-library cry of pleasure that she was sure could be heard for miles. When she finally recovered enough of her senses to open her eyes, Cait was watching her with the most devilishly sweet grin. Alex pulled her down and kissed her.

"I'm going to get you back for that."

Alex and Cait spent the weekend locked in Alex's apartment, getting acquainted on a whole new level. Alex never had such a good time going nowhere. And she'd never seen a sight quite as pleasing first thing in the morning as Cait, standing in her kitchen, sipping tea in nothing but the nightshirt she'd borrowed from Alex's closet.

"I hate that it's already Sunday," Alex said, wrapping her arms around Cait's waist and nuzzling her neck. Alex heard the clink of ceramic on stone as Cait set down her tea.

"The library's going to be so lonely without you," Cait whispered. She stroked the back of Alex's head, where Alex knew her hair was an absolute mess of tangles.

"I'll have to find excuses to visit," Alex whispered back. She kissed Cait's neck slowly, enjoying the sensation and taste of Cait's skin on her lips.

"I could visit you."

"Naw," Alex shook her head, burrowing her face deeper into Cait's inexplicably soft copper locks. "Meeting at the library is better. Much quieter. More privacy."

"Oh, okay."

"I'll text before I come by." Alex kissed Cait's neck again. Cait pulled back.

"I should probably head home soon," she said. Her voice returning to a more neutral, less 'bedroom' tone.

"Already?" Alex looked sadly at her. She pushed out her lip in a pout. "But I don't want you to go."

"You'll see me again," Cait smiled faintly.

"I'd better. I think I'm addicted." Alex grinned at her. "I can feel myself starting to go through withdrawal just thinking about you leaving. Withdrawal can be fatal, you know."

"I think you'll survive," Cait pulled away and began to gather up her things. Alex hated to see her go.

"How can you be certain? You are a pretty powerful drug, Cait Murphy."

"You'll just have to come to the library for your fix then." Cait finished dressing and gave Alex one last teasing goodbye kiss before disappearing out the door. Alex collapsed on her sofa. She couldn't remember the last time she'd been so happy in her life.

Chapter 20

"Oh, my word, as I live and breathe, is that Alex Rossi, back to claim her throne?" Charles teased as Alex waltzed back into her cube Monday morning with her box of office trinkets and a grin as wide as the Mississippi.

"Lesbian queen, back on the scene," Alex announced as she dropped the box on her desk. She sat down in her old office chair with a sigh. With one foot, she swiveled herself around, back and forth, appreciating the comfortable familiarity. Alex couldn't help but note the differences too. She'd changed in these months away. And sitting in that chair, Alex could feel that change.

"So, what's the scoop, your queerness?" Charles settled himself into the chair across from her on the other side of the desk. He steepled his fingers and raised his blonde eyebrows at her. "Tell me all about your latest misadventures."

"We tested the migration solution; it works but-"

"Oh, shut up, you know I don't mean with the project. I mean, with your hot librarian friend! I never got the follow-up, girl!" Charles leaned forward. "So? Did you get with her or not?"

"What do you think?" Alex said, elusively. She didn't really want to discuss Cait with Charles, but Charles was clearly expecting a story and wouldn't let it alone until he got *something* out of her.

"You did, didn't you?" Charles grinned. "Just the once or...?" He peered at her.

"You can never have just one," Alex shrugged and looked innocently away. Charles snorted and Alex looked back at him with a shrug. "Hey, I can't help it if women can't get enough of me." She wasn't about to give him sordid details; however a little vague bragging while letting him fill in the blanks himself seemed harmless enough. It's not like she was telling him anything personal about Cait.

"Was it good?" Charles prodded.

"Dude, it's *me*. I make everything good." Alex leaned back with a wry smile. She thought about the past weekend, and her whole body tingled. Cait was better than good; she was amazing. Charles laughed.

"Well, don't you look pleased with yourself," he said. "I know you said she was super hot, but I hope you're not too smitten. She is still a librarian, you know." Charles shook his head and clucked his tongue reproachfully. Alex remembered his warning from earlier, about Geoff blowing a fuse if he were to find out she was 'sleeping with the enemy.' Charles was a good friend, but not always the best secret-keeper. *It might be best if he believes it was just a fling.*

"Naw, don't worry," Alex feigned nonchalance. "You know what they say, what happens in the library, stays in the library." *I'll just wait until the migration plan is sorted. If that mess is settled, it shouldn't matter that I'm seeing a librarian.* "But I'm here now so…"

"So you stuck around long enough to bang the sexy librarian and then get transferred back? Nice work," Charles reached out for a high-five. Alex winced internally as she slapped his palm. She was being kind of gross, but it was just Charles, so she continued to play it cool.

"That's how I roll," Alex agreed.

"Lovely, Alex," Cait stepped around from the other side of the cube wall. God only knew how long she had been there. *Shit*. Alex froze. *What did she hear?* Enough, apparently. Cait's face was bright red as she shook her head and glared at Alex. "Just lovely. And silly me, I thought you actually cared."

"Cait! I.. I do," Alex insisted. "I just…"

"I'm gonna go…" Charles eased himself out of his chair. He looked sympathetically at Alex. "Sorry, bro," he whispered before slinking away.

"Cait, I'm sorry I didn't mean to…" Alex began. "This is all a misunderstanding."

"Is that why you didn't want me to visit you here?" Cait asked. Alex's head spun.

"What? I never said-"

"You said you'd rather come to me than the other way around. Did you not?" Cait's voice was pointed, her eyes burrowing into Alex's.

"No," *Did I?* Alex thought back to their last conversation before Cait had left her apartment. *Shit*. "I mean, I guess, technically, but I didn't mean it like that."

"Just like you didn't mean to tell your *bro* how you 'banged' the librarian?" Cait spat out bitterly. "Because that's all that I am to you, a *librarian* who's good for a ride?" Cait's voice was beginning to break. *She's going to cry.* Alex's guts clenched; she knew she'd fucked up, but her mind was blank with panic, and she didn't know how to fix it.

"No, I care about you, really." Alex could hear how unconvincing she sounded. Cait must have heard it too because she shook her head.

"If you care, this is some way to show it," she said. "I thought you were a kind person, Alex. But I don't deserve to be talked about like some *conquest*."

"I… I'm sorry, Cait. I didn't mean it like that. I just thought, well, with the migration I didn't want them to think that I-"

"That you could actually *give a fuck* about a librarian?" Cait scoffed. "But you can let them know you *fucked* one?"

"You're overreacting-" Alex knew she shouldn't have said that the moment it left her mouth. The pain in Cait's eyes was excruciating to see.

"Go to hell, Alex," Cait whispered before she turned and practically ran from the room.

"Cait, wait!" Alex jumped up to follow. Before she could get out the door, Geoff appeared. He stood in the doorway with another man in a suit, blocking Alex's path.

"Excuse me," Alex tried to push past them, but Geoff didn't move.

"Alex, I'm here to see you," he said. "I need to talk to you about the migration-"

"Can I just... can I get back to you? I just have this… situation," Alex looked desperately over Geoff's shoulder, but Cait had already disappeared.

"No, Alex, this cannot wait," Geoff said with firm impatience. "This is Dave Bigby. I don't know if you've met-"

"Yes, no, we haven't, hi," Alex said distractedly as she shook the large man's hand. She knew who Dave was. He was the VP above Geoff; he was Alex's uber-boss. And Alex couldn't have cared less at that moment. The only thing on her mind was finding Cait and repairing the absolute mess she had made of their relationship. *Fuck my big stupid mouth.*

"If you'll follow us to the conference room," Geoff said. Reluctantly Alex let Geoff lead her down the hall toward the conference room. As she walked, she pulled out her phone to text Cait.

'I'm so sorry, please can we talk?'

'No.' Cait texted back almost instantly.

Alex felt her throat constrict. *Come on, Cait, please?* Alex texted her again. This time she got no response. Alex barely registered that she'd entered the conference room until Geoff spoke, beckoning her to sit down.

"Dave and I would like to go over the latest details pertaining to the campus migration project," he said.

"Not the goddamn migration again," Alex grumbled under her breath as she slowly sat down in the seat beside Geoff, across the table from Dave. She texted Cait again.

'Please, I know I messed up. Please give me another chance.'

"Now, let's talk about this issue with the library," Geoff began.

"I've already told you how to fix that," Alex said, not looking up from her phone. *Come on, Cait, please.*

"We're going to go over it *again*," Geoff said through gritted teeth. He leaned closer to Alex. "Please watch your tone if you want to have a job at the end of this meeting," he hissed into her ear. Alex didn't fully process what he was saying because, at the same time, her phone buzzed with a message from Cait.

'Leave me alone. This is OVER. Enjoy being back HOME in your REAL JOB. Find somebody in the student union to BANG.'

"No, no, no," Alex whispered under her breath as she hurriedly texted Cait back.

'I don't want somebody else! This isn't just about sex! Really! I should never have said those things. I'm so sorry. Please give me another chance.'

'Don't bother texting me again, I'm blocking your number.'

Alex's throat felt so tight she could hardly breathe. *How did I fuck this up so quickly?* It had all happened so fast. One moment she was happy, she had Cait, she had her job back, and like an idiot, she'd thrown it away by bragging like some frat-guy asshole. Alex cursed herself, her stupid mouth, her stupid pride. Tears were threatening at the edges of her vision. *I have to go to the library.* She couldn't if she was stuck in this assinine meeting. *Why does Geoff always have the worst timing?* At that moment, Alex couldn't have cared less about CUIT, her job, and the damned migration project.

"Alex!" Geoff snapped. "If you would, *please* set down your phone and focus. Dave is here to sort this out-"

"There's nothing to sort out!" Alex interrupted sharply. "The project was a stupid over-reach that was always doomed to failure because you didn't consult with the library before making sweeping decisions-"

"Alex, it is wildly inappropriate to-" Geoff began, but Alex was out of patience for him and his overblown ego.

"It's 'inappropriate' to tell the truth?! You spent the last several months scapegoating me because of your fuck-up, but it's not my fault that your lack of forethought bit you in the ass. I came up with a solution. You have barely listened to me-"

"Alex, may I speak with you in private for a minute?" Geoff's neck was turning red, his jaw clenched in anger. Alex didn't care. She was furious with herself and fed up with him, and above all, she was terrified over the thought of losing Cait. Alex lost all control of her emotions.

"If you'd listened before, we wouldn't need this meeting!" Alex snapped at him.

"Now, Alex." Geoff all but dragged Alex into the deserted hallway. The act of standing and walking woke Alex up to the reality of what she'd just done. She'd been so upset about Cait that she'd just yelled at her boss. In front of *his* boss. *Shit. How many ways can I mess up my life in one day?*

"Look, I'm sorry about the meeting," Alex gritted her teeth as she tried to apologize to Geoff while the alarm bells over losing Cait continued to ring in her head.

"That was beyond unacceptable," Geoff scolded. Alex's phone buzzed, and she looked hopefully at the screen. It was Charles, not Cait. *I need to find Cait.* Alex ignored Charles' message and texted Cait again, vaguely aware as she did that Geoff was still talking to her. "Your behavior these last few months has caused more trouble for this department than… Are you even listening to me?"

"I said I'm sorry, but I just can't go over all this again right now," Alex replied tersely. "I need to deal with something. I think I just lost my girlfriend and I need to-"

"You just lost your job!" Geoff cut her off.

"What?" Alex felt her eyes go wide.

"Clean out your desk."

"But I just-"

"I'm calling security; they will escort you out of the building. You're done, Alex." Geoff was dead serious. Alex was too stunned to argue. It had all happened so quickly that none of it felt real. *How did this all happen at once? What the hell is going on with my life?*

When security arrived, she walked numbly back to her desk. Charles asked her what was going on, but all Alex could do was shake her head. She picked up her things and walked out of the student union. Security left her at her car. She shut herself inside and tried to process what had just happened. *I just lost my job.* She should be terrified; she should be pissed. She should *care.* But all she could think about was Cait.

Alex turned the key in the ignition. *I have to find her.*

Alex drove out to the edge of campus. Her heart pounded in her ears when she opened the big old library doors. Cait wasn't in her office. She wasn't at the circulation desk or the research desk. She wasn't in the archives. Alex texted her again. Nothing.

Come on, Cait. Where are you? Please talk to me. Alex combed the stacks looking for Cait. With every passing second, Alex grew more desperate and hopeless. The numbing shock of losing her job had worn off. She was breathing hard, tears spilling down her cheeks when she ran into Joan.

"Are you okay?" Joan asked, eyes wide with concern.

"Have you seen Cait?" Alex managed to ask as she tried to choke back her tears.

"She went home. She said she wasn't feeling well."

"Okay, thank you," Alex sniffled. She cried her way back through the stacks. She was half-blinded by tears, but it didn't matter; Alex could find her way around that library in her sleep now. *If I can't fix this, I may never walk through here again.* Alex sent Cait another desperate text. Then she texted Jenny.

'I lost my job and Cait hates me. I'm a wreck. Can I come over?'

'Oh shit, that sucks. Yeah, come on over!'

Chapter 21

Alex knew she must have looked like a complete mess when she walked through the door into Jenny's apartment. She couldn't remember the last time she'd cried that hard. It was messy, sloppy, crying. Her eyes stung, her throat was scratchy. Her nose was runny, and probably red. She wiped it on her sleeve again.

"I don't know what to do," Alex sobbed as she let herself fall onto the sofa. She burrowed under Jenny's afghan. "I've fucked it all up."

"You'll find a new job in no time at all," Jenny sat beside her. "You're so good with computers-"

"No, not about my job. Fuck my job," Alex shook her head. "What am I going to do about Cait?"

"Cait, the hot librarian?" Jenny tilted her head and looked quizzically at Alex. "I thought you were just hooking up. I didn't know it was a thing."

Alex took a few deep breaths so that she could speak without crying.

"I thought so too at first, but then… last weekend…" Alex put her face in her hands. It was all so confusing. "It felt like a relationship, but I guess I wasn't really sure... We never really talked about it, like in words. I wanted to ask her if she was my girlfriend but every time I'd try to bring it up, we'd just end up…"

"Fucking?" Jenny snorted. Alex groaned.

"I wanted it to be more, but I didn't know what she wanted…" Alex had replayed every moment of the last few weeks over in her head. Alex had intended to ask Cait the relationship question. But they hadn't actually gotten to it. They were too lost in the moments together. *I was too chickenshit to say it out loud.*

"So, wait, back up. Why does she hate you?" Jenny still looked perplexed. Alex sighed and sat up, arranging the afghan around herself like a shawl.

"She overheard me talking to Charles. And I was being kind of… well, you know how I am with

Charles. He's like my bro. I don't talk to him about mushy things like feelings. I was just like, yeah, I banged her…" She felt a twist of guilt, thinking back to the way she'd described Cait these last few months; she'd discussed her like a prize to be won, a challenge to be conquered. Not a wonderful caring person who deserved kindness and decency.

"That's why she's mad? Because you were bro-ing out?" Jenny sighed. "I mean, that's not cool, but was it really 'never speak to me again' terrible?"

"There might have been a high-five." Alex put her face in her hands.

"Oh?"

"I was being so gross." Alex felt sick about it. She was as bad as those assholes on the street, whistling at her and Cait for kissing. Their relationship, physical or otherwise, shouldn't have been used for entertainment. "I was really just trying to act cool… I never thought she'd hear me."

"Not a great excuse…"

"It's worse than that," Alex said. "I care about her, I want to be with her. But for some stupid reason, I acted like I didn't. I made it sound like I was gonna hit it and quit it now that I was back in the student union."

"But you don't want to hit it quit it? You wanted to stay and play?" Jenny trying to hide a smile, but she wasn't doing a very good job.

"Shut up," Alex groaned and put her face in her hands again.

"Oh, come on, you started it, *bro*," Jenny whacked her with a pillow cushion.

"Leave me alone. Can't you see I'm heartbroken here?" Alex shoved the cushion back in Jenny's face.

"Heartbroken?" Jenny repeated, eyebrows raised. "Are you in love with her?"

"No, I didn't mean it like that," Alex shook her head.

"Oh, really? What the hell else does 'heartbroken' mean?" Jenny stared at her. *What did I mean?* Alex crossed held her arms across her belly and poked at the feeling inside of herself. *I can't be in love with her. Can I?*

"It's just that… when I think about being without her, it's like somebody's literally stabbing me in the chest." Alex squeezed herself tighter, tears once more at the corners of her eyes. "It hurts. It's killing me how much it hurts."

"That kind of sounds like you're in love with her," Jenny said. The truth of it hit Alex like a Mack truck.

"Oh, god, I am." Alex curled into the fetal position and started to cry again. *I love her. I love her, and I lost her without ever asking how she really felt about me.*

"Shhh, Alex, it's okay," Jenny squeezed her shoulder. Alex shook her head.

"But I messed it all up…" Alex whimpered. "Oh, god. What am I going to do?"

"Uh, go win her back?" Jenny said, as if 'winning her back' were as easy as picking up a carton of milk at the grocery store.

"How can I?" Alex sniffed. "She's not answering my texts. She said she'd block my number. I looked for her at the library… I don't even know where she lives, and now I'm locked out of the university system I can't even look it up!"

"But you know where she works," Jenny pointed out.

"Yeah, but when I went to her office, she wasn't there. And I don't know when she'll be back. What am I going to do? Stakeout the library?" Alex shook her head.

"Why not?"

"Geoff already had security walk me out of the student union after he fired me. When the librarians find out I was fired, they'll drive me out of the library like a convicted witch. They aren't going to let me hang around to harass one of their own."

"Really?" Jenny looked dubious. "They're *librarians*. What would they even do? Librarians are like... fluffy little kittens."

"With pointy little claws." Alex shuddered. "Haven't you ever heard of cat-scratch fever? Even fluffy little kittens can be dangerous, you know."

"Psht, sounds like you already have Cait-scratch fever," Jenny said with a snort.

"You're choosing to pun at a time like this?"

"You walked right into that one," Jenny laughed. Alex scowled. Jenny pushed her lightly. "Come on," she said. "I'm just trying to lift your spirits."

"I think *spirits* would lift my spirits better," Alex retorted.

"I can help with that!" Jenny got up and went to the cupboard. "So what will it be? It sounds like you have a taste for the Irish these days." Jenny licked her lips suggestively. "How about a taste of Irish whiskey?"

"Fuck you," Alex said, although she couldn't help but smile, just a little.

"So that's a pass on the whiskey then? Too bad... Does Cait like it?"

"I don't know, I've never had whiskey with Cait." Alex looked curiously at Jenny. "Why's that 'too bad'?"

"Markus really wants a whiskey tasting buddy, it drives him nuts that I only drink the cheap stuff in mixed drinks. But I just can't drink it straight. Even the 'good stuff.' It all tastes like painful dirt to me..." Jenny started to mix Alex one of her favorite self-pity drinks: rum and *Coke*, light on the *Coke*. "If you do win Cait back, you'll have to ask her. Then we could go to those things together, us with our mixed drinks, them with their spicy dirt water."

"What are you going on about?" Alex asked, staring dumbly at her best friend. "Are you planning a double-date? Seriously? She's not even talking to me, remember?"

"I know, I know. Call me an optimist, but I think you can get her back." Jenny sat beside Alex and handed her the drink.

"You say optimism, I say false hope." Alex took a big gulp of the strong drink. It burned good; Alex felt her body begin to relax almost immediately.

"Whatever, fine. I'll switch to trying to take your mind off her, okay?" Jenny pulled out her phone. "Come on, let's get drunk and play *Heads-Up*."

Alex shook her head. She didn't have the energy for playing a game, even she and Jenny's most favorite giggle-inducing one.

"I'm not going to forget about her that easily. I'll get drunk; I just can't..." Alex felt tears welling up again, and she took another big gulp to force them down. "I just can't be so… optimistic. But I'm not giving up yet, you know."

"I don't want you to give up, Alex," Jenny assured her. "But if you aren't going hole-up in the library and wait for her, then it's my job as your best friend to get you drunk and distracted for a while. Come on, we haven't watched *Clueless* in forever."

"Thanks," Alex said gratefully. Jenny smiled and thumped her on the back.

Natalie Falkenwrath

"What are best friends for?"

Chapter 22

Alex let Jenny get her absolutely *tanked*. Luckily Jenny didn't have any classes the next day until late in the afternoon. So Alex and Jenny stayed up until the wee hours of the morning playing *Heads-Up*, watching nineties throwback movies, and gorging themselves on booze and pizza bagels. Any time Alex would start feeling the sharp pangs of heartache, Jenny would refill her drink. It was a good distraction. However, as a result, Alex spent the majority of the day on Tuesday laying on Jenny's sofa nursing a rum-and-regret hangover. She was in no condition to go back to the library to win Cait over.

By the time Alex finally got herself back to her own apartment, her headache had eased, but the sense of remorse and longing had grown twice as strong. Alex looked at the clock. It was too late to go back in search of Cait. *Tomorrow. I will go in and talk to her tomorrow.* The minutes ticked by slowly as Alex waited for the day to end. It felt like an eternity. She showered and forced herself to eat a decent dinner. All the while, the only thing she could think about was Cait. All she saw when she closed her eyes was that familiar copper hair and fair face.

Alex felt her body physically throb from the anguish of missing her. Her arms felt empty without Cait in them, her lips ached hungrily for her kisses. The thought that she might never kiss her again filled Alex with a hollowness that seemed to consume her whole being. Unable to stand the loneliness any longer, Alex took some sleeping pills and went to bed early.

The next morning, Alex was wide awake long before her alarm went off. She dressed quickly, her whole body vibrating with nervous energy in anticipation of seeing Cait. Alex went to put her hair in its usual ponytail but, remembering what Cait had said, left it down. She brushed out her brown waves until her hair shone. Alex looked in the mirror. She was hardly a match for Cait, but she didn't look terrible either. The sleep had helped. Her eyes were no longer bloodshot from crying. *Let's keep it that way, Alexandria Rossi,* she told herself.

The drive to the university felt surreal. If Alex didn't win Cait back today, she might lose her forever. That pressure put Alex's mind into a fog of 'what if's. *What if she won't even talk to me?* Alex's heart pounded heavily in her chest as she walked up to the big old library doors. It was bitter cold outside, and her whole body was shaking with chill and nerves. And yet she couldn't make herself reach for the handle. *Just go in. Do it.*

Before Alex could work up the courage, a pair of students pushed the doors open from within. One of them held the door for her, and Alex was forced by social niceties to put one foot in front of the other and walk into the library. Cait's library.

Alex stood just inside the entrance for a moment while her eyes adjusted to the dim light. Manny, the man-brarian, was at the circulation desk. Alex walked past him. Joan, Cait's officemate, was at the research desk; Alex walked past her, as well. With Joan at the desk, it meant that if Cait were in her office, she'd be alone. Alex slipped into the stacks before Joan noticed her. If *anybody* knew that she and Cait were at odds,

Joan would know. Alex wasn't ready to discuss it with Joan.

Alex wove her way towards Cait's office. The door was closed - Alex knocked. She held her breath, waiting. There was no answer - she knocked again.

"Cait?" Alex called out quietly.

"She's not there," Nancy's voice behind her made Alex yelp in surprise.

"Oh, you scared me," Alex put a hand over her pounding heart.

"I'm sorry, I didn't mean to sneak up on you," said Nancy.

"That's okay. Do you know where Cait is?"

"I think she's in the archives," Nancy said pleasantly. Alex thanked her and started off in the direction of the archives. As she walked, she thought about Nancy's demeanor - she'd been as friendly as ever, not curious, or hostile. It was totally business-as-usual. *Geoff hasn't told the library he fired me yet.* Alex was sure of it. *That means Cait probably doesn't know.*

Alex found Cait at the back of the archives, sitting at the very table she had once pulled Alex onto in the heat of passion. Her head was lowered, and Alex couldn't see her face. She was dressed in the same green sweater and tan skirt she'd been wearing the first time Alex had ever laid eyes on her. Back then, Alex's first thought was that Cait's body was made for lingerie. Now Alex knew that Cait was best suited to wearing nothing at all. Remembered images floated through Alex's mind. Cait lying naked beside her in bed, running her fingers along Alex's skin, as they talked about everything from family to movies to childhood pets. That weekend had been so special, so perfectly wonderful. They'd been lost in a world all their own. *I have to get that back; I have to get her back.*

Alex watched Cait for a moment while she worked up the courage to speak. Cait had such intense focus when she was reading. Alex loved that about her; she loved everything she knew about Cait, and she wanted to learn more. Cait absently stroked her long red hair, the way she did it made Alex jealous of Cait's own slender fingers. *Don't mess this up, or you'll never touch her again.* Alex wished that she'd thought to bring a gift, flowers, something to show that her apologies were serious and heartfelt. Too late. *Words will have to do.*

"Cait?" Alex stepped up to the table. Cait jumped to her feet.

"Alex, what are you doing here?" Cait's tone was immediately cold and hostile. She crossed her arms and frowned at Alex.

"Can I just talk to you?" Alex felt her heart in her throat. "Please?"

"You shouldn't be here. You don't work in the library anymore," Cait said coolly.

"I don't work *anywhere* anymore," replied Alex.

"What do you mean?"

"I mean, I was fired," Alex confessed. "I am no longer an employee of Cowling University."

"Why were you fired?" Cait asked slowly, tilting her head to look suspiciously at Alex. Alex felt her cheeks burn.

"My stupid mouth, what else?" Alex shrugged deep into her shoulders. Talking about losing her job was embarrassing, and it wasn't what she'd come here to discuss. *But of course, Cait would want to know why*. Alex took a deep breath. "I kinda told Geoff off... about the migration... in front of his boss. So, he fired me."

"I'm sorry to hear that," Cait said, although there was no empathy in her voice. She was still giving Alex a cold look.

"I don't even care. That's not why I'm here. I'm here for you." Alex took Cait's hand.

"Are you then?" Cait wrenched her hand away. "Come back to 'bang the librarian' again, have you?"

"No," Alex shook her head firmly. "Cait, I'm sorry. It wasn't right for me to talk about you like that-"

"No, it wasn't," Cait snapped.

"I know! I'm so incredibly sorry. It's killing me that I hurt you." Alex felt her voice begin to crack, and she swallowed. She didn't want to cry. She took deep, slow breaths as she searched Cait's eyes for any hint of forgiveness.

"So, you came here to apologize then?" Cait asked, looking away as if bored. But Alex could see the hints of emotion that Cait was trying to hide in the way her lips pressed together and her eyes blinked rapidly as if holding back tears. These signs gave Alex a faint glimmer of hope that Cait might care about her enough to give her another chance.

"I came here to get you back."

"I don't want to be your workplace conquest, Alex," Cait said. Her voice had lost some of its edge.

"You aren't. You never were. I mean, I didn't know what you were. But you never could have been just a… conquest." Alex stared hard at Cait, willing her to understand. "If that's how I felt, if that's the kind of person I was, I wouldn't have stopped you when you kissed me while I was still with Jasmine. No matter what stupid shit I say to Charles, that's not the kind of person I am. Conquests and hook-ups aren't the kind of thing I want."

"Then why talk like that at all?!"

"I don't know!" Alex squeaked. "Because I'm an insecure idiot! Because I didn't know what you wanted, and I was scared to ask!"

"What?"

"I was afraid if I asked you to be my girlfriend, you'd laugh at me."

"Alex-"

"I was afraid that *you* might have only been looking for a hook-up, and I was reading too much into things. I mean, you came onto me in a bathroom-"

"That was ages ago!" Cait interrupted. "Come on, Alex! That's a shite excuse! We'd moved beyond shifting in bathrooms. I thought that was quite clear when we spent all fucking weekend together. The way we talked... I thought you cared about me."

"Jesus Cait, I don't just care about you! I *love* you!"

The air in Alex's lungs seemed to freeze, refusing to let her breathe as she watched the expression on Cait's face. *Does she believe me?* Cait's eyes were wide, her lips parted, but she wasn't saying anything. *What if she doesn't love me back?* Alex dropped her eyes to her feet.

"I'm sorry," Alex whispered. "I can't blame you if you don't want anything to do with me, but I guess I was hoping that maybe-"

"Shut up and kiss me, Alex."

Alex looked up. Cait's eyes were shining with unshed tears, her perfect lips curled in a soft smile. Alex didn't need to be told twice. She took Cait's face in her hands and kissed her. Their kisses were soft and sweet at first, but soon they were devouring each other. *Shifting.* And every cell in Alex's body seemed fit to burst with joy. She pulled Cait closer.

"Ah-hem," a voice behind them made Alex and Cait spring apart. Nancy was standing at the entrance to the archives. Blood rushed to Alex's face; it burned in painful embarrassment at being caught. Nancy didn't scold them, she only smirked as she told Cait that Mandy was waiting in her office.

"Tell her I'll be right there, I just need to *talk* with Alex a moment," Cait said.

"Mandy wants to see Alex, too," Nancy added.

"Me? She does?" Alex forgot her embarrassment in favor of confusion. W*hy would the library director want to see me?* Alex wondered if she was in trouble for returning to the library after she'd been fired.

"I don't know," Nancy shook her head. Cait shrugged at Alex, and they followed Nancy out of the archives.

"I can't believe she caught us," Alex whispered.

"I'm honestly kind of surprised we hadn't gotten caught before," Cait whispered back. She smiled wickedly. "At least this time, we had all of our clothing on."

Mandy was sitting in the chair next to Cait's desk when the pair arrived. Alex had no inkling of what to expect from the library director. *Am I in trouble? How could I be in more trouble than already being fired? Oh, shit, is Cait in trouble?* Alex would hate herself if she'd somehow managed to tank both her career and Cait's in one terrible stroke.

"Mandy, good to see you. What can we do for you?" Cait greeted Mandy politely and settled into her desk chair. Alex pulled a third chair over from next to Joan's desk and sat awkwardly beside Cait.

"I was informed this morning that Alex had been released from her position at CUIT," Mandy began. *Released? That's a nice word for it.*

"Yeah, Geoff… let me go… earlier this week," Alex confirmed.

"I need to know where that leaves us with regards to this forced migration," Mandy continued. "I don't feel comfortable going ahead with any updates without the assurances you had given us, Alex. If you're no longer with the university, is there another tech that I'll have to deal with?"

"Uh, I don't know really... Last I talked to Geoff, he was bringing Dave Bigby into the conversation."

"Well, that's fucking fantastic," Mandy snorted. Alex and Cait both sat up, shocked. They looked at each other with amazement at hearing this serious, professional woman say such a thing.

"Is that a problem then?" Cait asked cautiously. Mandy shook her head.

"It means I'm only left with one option. And Dave knows it." Mandy's eyes narrowed dangerously.

"What's that?" Alex asked, unable to hide her curiosity. Mandy shook her head again.

"If Geoff can't work with me without running to *daddy*, I can't work with him. At all." Mandy said. "Alex, could you implement some version of your solution without the backing of CUIT?"

"Uh, I mean, yeah, I guess. It would be different, a little, and I'd need to, you know, work here… but technically… yeah, I think so," Alex stammered.

"Alright. Well, I think that's all I can say for now. I'll be in touch," Mandy said. She gave Alex an expectant look. Slowly Alex rose from her chair. She was thoroughly confused, but it seemed clear enough that Mandy was dismissing her.

"Okay… Uh, talk to you later," Alex looked pleadingly at Cait.

"I'll call you," Cait promised. She gave Alex a small, secretive smile, and something inside of Alex relaxed. She still had no clue as to what was going on with Mandy and the library. And she was still unemployed. But she'd gotten Cait back. And that was all that truly mattered to her.

Alex wandered out through the library's large front doors into the crisp winter air. She took a deep breath and exhaled, watching as it formed a frosty cloud in front of her. *What do I do now?* Alex's phone vibrated.

'I'm not going to be able to see you until after work, meet at the Union Tap later?' Cait's text said.

'Sure, what time?' Alex replied.

'5:01. I promise not to be late this time.'

Alex smiled. She shoved her phone in her pocket and walked back to her car. She was still jobless and had all day. *Might as well accomplish something.* She hopped in her car and drove to the mall.

It was humbling to return to her former employer at the computer store and ask for her old job back. But Alex knew it would be the easiest and fastest way to be employed once more. They agreed to interview her on the spot.

'What are you up to?' Cait texted.

'Trying to get my old job at the mall back.'

'Don't bother, Mandy and I had a better idea.' Cait's text didn't give Alex any reason. Alex scratched her head.

'Why? Are you sure?' Alex wondered if it would be foolish to throw away a chance at her old job. Even if she'd hated this job, she needed to pay rent, and they seemed eager enough to give her a chance.

'Trust me. Forget the Union Tap. Go home. I'll see you there later tonight.'

Alex took a deep breath. *Trust her. I can do that.*

She apologized to the store manager and returned to her apartment. She tidied up in anticipation of Cait's arrival. When the apartment was clean, Alex settled into playing video games. She'd lost track of time, and when she heard a knock on the door was shocked that it was already after seven in the evening.

"Hello, Alex," Cait smiled as Alex opened the door to let her in. "I'm sorry I took so long, but I wanted to get a few things." She was wearing her long black winter coat and green scarf. Her knees were bare, and her stiletto heels seemed impractical for the snow.

"Get what few things?" Alex asked, eyeing Cait with confusion. Cait's empty hands were cold when they touched Alex's face.

"How about a job for starters?"

"You got me a job?" Alex asked. "Did you get me my old job back? How?"

"I did you one better. A job working directly for the director of university libraries. No more CUIT, no more Geoff. Mandy will be calling you in the morning."

"What? How?"

"The best part is," Cait continued, ignoring Alex's stunned questions. She pulled out Alex's ponytail and twirled her fingers through her hair. "You get your choice of libraries in which to work. There are many fine libraries at Cowling University, you know. You could be wherever-"

"Yours." Alex interrupted. "I want to be with you." Cait smiled. "I always want to be with you."

"I'm glad you want to be with me, Alex. Because that means I can give you something else…" Cait took a step back and unbuttoned her coat. Alex's breath caught short as Cait revealed her body, dressed in sheer black lingerie. Alex greedily took in the sight of her, as heat crackled like lightning through her veins.

Alex approached her wordlessly - for no words could possibly have captured the splendor of Cait or the feeling she evoked within Alex. She ran her hands softly up Cait's bare arms, and across her collar bones. Her fingers lightly traced the black straps of Cait's risqué attire - over her shoulders, across her chest, and down between her breasts. Cait shivered, and Alex watched her nipples harden under the all-but-transparent fabric.

As Alex continued her meticulous inspection of Cait's scantily clad body, Cait began to undress her, unbuttoning her shirt, unbuckling her belt. Cait knelt to help Alex out of her pants. While down there, she placed a kiss between Alex's legs, her breath felt hot through the cotton fabric of Alex's underwear. Alex shuddered as her arousal intensified. *How did I get lucky enough to find this amazing woman? Does she know how amazing she is?*

"Cait," Alex pulled Cait to her feet and looked earnestly into her moss-green eyes.

"Yes, Alex?"

"I have never been as happy as I am when I am with you, I have never felt as desired or as valued. I love you, Cait. I love you, and I appreciate you - not just because you're the hottest fucking woman on the planet, which you *so* are, but because of everything that makes you, you. You're smart and funny and just... utterly amazing. I love all of you. And I want you to know that."

Alex could feel her heart thundering against her ribs. Back at the library, Alex had told Cait she'd loved her, and Cait had responded by kissing her. Cait hadn't said it back. Alex searched Cait's expression, yearning to hear those three words.

Cait smiled faintly and stroked Alex's cheek. *What if she doesn't love me?* She'd said they were beyond just a physical relationship, and that she cared. But was it love? Cait continued to look at her, silently. She touched Alex's face, tucked her hair behind her ears, and said nothing.

"Do you love me?" Alex blurted out when she could stand it no longer. "Or maybe, do you think you could love me? One day?" Alex amended. She didn't want to scare Cait away, this wasn't some love-me-or-else ultimatum. Alex just needed to know where she stood. "I'm sorry, I don't mean to-"

"It's okay, Alex. It's just... I've never told somebody… that," Cait admitted softly. "People have said it to me, but I never truly believed them. It was about sex in the end, it seems. I think maybe I use sex to keep people at a certain length. But somehow, you got under my skin…" Cait took a deep breath. "That is a long, convoluted way to say, yes, Alex. I love you."

Alex nearly choked on her own happy tears. Before she could get caught crying, Alex pulled Cait in and kissed her. Cait kissed her back with an intensity that turned Alex's blood to lava - molten hot and sparking fire wherever it flowed. The heat burned hottest in her heart and between her legs. Alex needed Cait, and she needed her *now*. Somehow they made their way to the bedroom and fell together into bed. The pressure of Cait's body on hers had never felt so satisfying. It wasn't just sex, it was *making love*. Alex hated the term, but there she was, her body and heart crying out in joy and pleasure in harmony with Cait's, and she knew no other way to describe it.

"So, does this mean you're officially my girlfriend now?" Alex asked once they'd collapsed panting and sweaty into each other's arms. Cait's shoulders shook as she laughed.

"I should hope so," she said.

"This might sound cliché, but… would you like to move in with me?" Alex asked. "Not right away," she rushed to add. "I just… I wonder if that's the kind of direction you see us moving in."

"Yes, Alex, I think I would, one day, very much like to live with you." Cait kissed her bare shoulder. Alex felt warm all over.

"You have no idea how happy that makes me," she said.

"Well, you're grinning like an *eejit*, so I have some idea," Cait teased.

"Shut up," Alex nudged her before letting out a long, contented sigh. "I love you, Cait."

"I love you too, Alex."

Chapter 23

It took over a month for Mandy to get all the paperwork and funding in order, but it was well worth the wait. Alex was hired directly under Mandy, in a new role built just for her. Alex was even encouraged to work with Cait to craft a job description that best suited Alex's talents and interests. And when it was all worked out, Alex couldn't have imagined a better position. Alex had never been as excited to go to work as she was on her first day back at the Cowling Library for the Humanities.

"I still can't believe you were able to do this for me," Alex said as she unpacked her box of trinkets once more in her small library office. CUIT had reclaimed all of Alex's Hackers-style monitor display. She was left with a simple laptop, the same base machine given to all university employees who didn't work in the tech department.

"We didn't do it for you, Alex. I keep telling you. We did it for us. We needed a brilliant in-house tech geek such as yourself." Cait watched her with a small, teasing smile. Alex rolled her eyes.

"Yeah, the brilliant idiot that got fired and caused an entire internal split." Alex stuck out her tongue and blew a raspberry. In the process of creating this new job for her, the library broke off from CUIT almost entirely.

"Ah, you give yourself too much credit," Cait shook her head, her copper hair sweeping over her shoulder. "The cracks in that foundation had been there all along. You just drew attention to them."

"Yeah, and stomped on them until the whole thing shifted and fell."

"Ah, well, I know how much you like *shifting*." Cait closed the door to Alex's office and locked it behind her. She pulled Alex into a deep kiss. "Welcome back." Cait kissed her again.

"I thought you didn't like 'shifting' in my office," Alex said with a grin.

"That was before when you had that monstrous display watching over us." Cait reached over and shut Alex's laptop. "Now, I believe I can do anything I want to do to you in here." Cait pulled Alex in tight and kissed her until Alex's knees began to weaken. There was a knock at the door.

"But maybe some other time," Cait winked. She opened the door, and a gaggle of librarians piled in - all there to welcome Alex back with hugs and handshakes. It was a little overwhelming, but overall it filled Alex with a warm sense of belonging.

"There's cake and tea in the break room!" Manny announced, and they all filed back out of the tiny closet-like office.

"Did you know about this?" Alex asked Cait as they followed the crowd. Cait took Alex by the hand.

"Who do you think picked out the cake?" Cait winked.

As Alex ate her cake, she realized the break room no longer felt bleak and cold. The walls were still gray, the couch ugly, and the chairs mismatched. But Alex had found a home there, at the library, and that made all the difference.

A year ago, Alex could never have imagined this; she'd settled for 'good enough,' and that was that. Alex would never have imagined that being moved to the library would be the first step in a domino effect that would leave her feeling happier than she had ever been in her adult life.

Alex smiled at Cait. *Banished to the library, lost in the stacks, found in love.*